## Plunging into the Depths

Mindy rolled up the right sleeve of her red flannel shirt. When she reached the fish tank, she held her nose, closed her eyes, and then plunged her arm into the slimy depths. She felt one goldfish touch her wrist as it swam by. Another gave her a quick little fishy kiss near the elbow.

It took a few moments of searching through the sand and pebbles to find the hair in the seaweed. Finally she yanked the tattered, tangled, and twisted toupee from the tank. Everyone cheered—including Mr. Finelli.

Mindy walked over to the teacher's desk and handed Mr. Finelli his dripping hair. It was one of the most humiliating moments in her life.

"Thank you." Mr. Finelli took the sopping-wet toupee from Mindy and immediately plopped it onto his head. As the green water trickled down his face, Mr. Finelli smiled and said, "Class dismissed."

# What Is the Teacher's Toupee Doing in the Fish Tank?

## Jerry Piasecki

A Skylark Book

New York • Toronto • London • Sydney • Auckland

RL 4.0, 008–012

WHAT IS THE TEACHER'S TOUPEE DOING IN THE FISH TANK?
A Skylark Book / December 1994

Skylark Books is a registered trademark of Bantam Books,
a division of Bantam Doubleday Dell Publishing Group, Inc.
Registered in the U.S. Patent and Trademark Office and elsewhere.

ISBN 0-553-48171-1

*Published simultaneously in the United States and Canada*

Bantam Books are published by Bantam Books, a division of Bantam
Doubleday Dell Publishing Group, Inc. Its trademark, consisting of
the words "Bantam Books" and the portrayal of a rooster, is
Registered in U.S. Patent and Trademark Office and in other
countries. Marca Registrada. Bantam Books, 1540 Broadway,
New York, New York 10036.

PRINTED IN THE UNITED STATES OF AMERICA

OPM          0 9 8 7 6 5 4 3 2

# What Is the Teacher's Toupee Doing in the Fish Tank?

# Chapter One

**At Doverton School** there were all sorts of rumors about what went on in Mr. Finelli's classroom. The shades were always drawn, and a DO NOT DISTURB—LEARNING IN PROGRESS sign stayed hung on the door. But no one who'd been assigned to Mr. Finelli's classroom would ever talk about what actually happened behind that door. It was as if they were part of some secret club, and sworn to silence. That's probably what scared the other students the most. Once someone entered Finelli-ville, he or she was never the same again.

Mr. Finelli himself was as thin as a string of red licorice, and his skin was dark beige. He was about six foot two, but he appeared shorter because he always slouched. His brown hair was so tangled that it looked like he'd left it out all night on a flagpole during a hurricane. Word was that he combed it once a year, on the first day of school, though it never seemed to matter; the hair on top of his head didn't quite match the hair on the sides. He always wore the same old brown suit, which looked like it had spent the night with his hair.

Mr. Finelli had almost no lips, and his large nose was crooked from being broken. Whenever someone asked what had caused it, he'd say it was from "an old blowing injury."

But the one thing that struck everyone about Mr. Finelli was his eyes. They shone like polished black marbles under his bushy eyebrows. When Mr. Finelli looked at you, you could swear he was seeing into your very soul.

Each year the worst, nastiest, meanest, toughest-to-teach teacher-torturing students were assigned to Mr. Finelli. This year one of them was named Mindy Collins.

Mindy was one of several sixth-graders who had been forced to transfer to Doverton School from other schools in the district. Her last, and most unforgivable, crime at her old school had been tying the women's and men's faculty bathroom doors together with her super-long jump rope.

On the day she picked to carry out her plan, it just

so happened that Principal Annabell Kelly and Vice Principal Stanley Korn had both stopped in the faculty lounges to, shall we say, take care of personal principal business. Mindy had no idea who was inside when she tied the doorknobs together and made several tight knots. But anyone who happened to be there was trapped. The doors were now impossible to open from the inside.

Shortly after Mindy knotted her final knot, the last bell rang and the school day was over.

It wasn't until seven-fifteen the next morning, when Mrs. Buckley, the gym teacher, arrived, that Mrs. Kelly and Mr. Korn were freed from their john-jails. It took Ms. Buckley forty-five minutes to untie the knots.

After spending a night on cold, hard tile the principal and vice principal were not happy campers. Because of her track record of tricks, Mindy was immediately a prime suspect. It didn't help her defense when she said, "It could have been worse, you know."

"How?" Principal Kelly asked, while picking out from her hair pieces of the toilet-paper ball she'd used for a pillow.

Mindy shrugged. "Well . . ." She thought for a moment and then snapped her fingers. "I know—today could have been Saturday!" Mindy started to giggle. She knew she shouldn't, but she just couldn't help it. Soon after that final giggle Mindy was gone.

Three other students assigned to Mr. Finelli's class had also just joined the Doverton student body. Not one of them had done so by choice. The school district made the decision for Jeff Graylin after he'd read Maureen McCauley's diary out loud—over the school P.A. Samantha Rison got her ticket to Doverton by replacing all the red paint in art with ketchup, the yellow with mustard, and the brown with homestyle beef gravy. Frankie Butler's only problem was that he liked to hit people.

The rest of the class was made up of Doverton originals who, because of either their behavior or a stroke of very bad luck, ended up being assigned to Mr. Finelli.

That first day of school in Room 201 started out pretty much the same as any other first day in any other classroom. While Mr. Finelli tried to take attendance, Samantha thought about her just completed summer vacation; Jeff slouched down so low that he slid to the floor and had to scramble to regain his seat and his cool; Frankie ground his teeth and cracked his knuckles; and Mindy tried to fight an attack of boredom by tapping out a tune on her desk with a pencil.

Mindy hadn't heard the rumors about Mr. Finelli, but it wouldn't have made any difference. When Mindy Collins got bored trouble always followed. And this morning, she decided that she hadn't been this bored since her dad made her watch golf on TV.

From her desk all Mindy could see was Mr. Finelli's messy hair sticking out above the huge seating chart he was reading. "And I'm supposed to stay awake?" Mindy whispered softly to herself. "Yeah, like, right."

Just after Mr. Finelli called out Frieda Jackson's name, Mindy let out the loudest yawn ever heard in the continental United States. Actually it sounded like it was only part yawn. It was also part burp, belch, and bellow. Mindy even impressed herself. I'll have to remember that one for Sunday school, she decided.

The entire class was momentarily stunned. Everyone stared at Mindy. No one said a word until Mindy, very quietly and sweetly, whispered in a super-high, squeaky voice: "Oppsy, dupsy, pupsy. Please excuse me, Mr. Fin-jelly."

At that point the class in Room 201 gave up its membership in the civilized world.

Everyone except Mr. Finelli started to laugh. He kept reading the names on the seating chart as if nothing out of the ordinary was happening. Meanwhile books flew, desks toppled, and several people rolled on the floor. Two students broke open their lunches and started sword fighting with Twinkies. Frankie Butler just walked around the room hitting people. The mayhem continued for exactly forty-two seconds. Then everyone heard the splash.

# Chapter Two

**Before the sound,** Frankie Butler had seen Mr. Finelli's toupee soaring through the air like a furry Frisbee. And Samantha had been distracted from hurling a marshmallow when something brown and hairy grazed her ear.

Now every sixth-grader in the room was watching their teacher's toupee sink slowly to the bottom of the huge fish tank. Goldfish were darting for cover, and even the snails seemed to be in shock as the hairpiece wove in with the green seaweed.

Jeff thought it would take ten minutes for that curly hunk of hair to make it to the bottom of the tank. Mindy thought its trip down would last forever. It was as if the whole class had been hypnotized.

It wasn't until the toupee came to rest on the layer

of pebbles at the bottom of the tank and the water cleared that the mood was broken by Mr. Finelli's slightly raspy voice. "That proves it once and for all . . . hair can't swim."

Everyone turned toward the front of the room. "Oh . . . my," Mindy gasped. Now instead of a bushy mass of brown hair poking up over the seating chart, the students saw an incredibly shiny bald head. All at once the head sank lower and disappeared. There was a long moment of absolute silence. Then a low noise came from behind the chart. Mr. Finelli had started to chant.

"Baa-bum. Baa-bum. Baa-bum." His voice was soft, low, and deep. A second later the chart began to sink slowly toward the desk. "Baa-bum. Baa-bum. Baa-bum. Baa-bum." The teacher's voice got louder, faster, and stronger as more of his face came into view from behind the chart.

Mr. Finelli's chanting started to fill the room. "Baa-bum! BAA-BUM! **BAA-BUM!**" Finally, when the chart was below his chin, Mr. Finelli jumped up from his chair, hopped over his desk, and raced over to Mindy. "*BAAAAAAAAAAA-BUM-BUM-BUM-BUM-BUM-BUM-BUM-BUM-BUM!*"

Mindy screamed.

Mr. Finelli smiled. He leaned over Mindy's desk until their noses were only an inch apart. "Hi,

Mindy," he said in a super-friendly voice. "Welcome to my class. Will you be so kind as to do me a favor?"

Mindy's eyes darted to the left and the right. Her classmates were frozen in shock. No one had ever seen a teacher act this way, or move that fast. Actually, Frankie thought, it would have been kind of cool—if only it wasn't a teacher who'd done it.

Mindy didn't answer Mr. Finelli's question, so he moved in closer. Now he was almost close enough for their eyelashes to bat high fives. "Just one itty-bitty favor?" Mr. Finelli said sweetly. "Paaaaaaaa-leeeeese."

*What a total geekoid*, Mindy thought. "Ooooooo-kay," Mindy said, mocking the way Mr. Finelli was speaking. "But only because you said 'Paaaaaaaa-leeeeese.' "

"Great." Mr. Finelli jumped up and walked back toward his desk. "In light of the fact that you started these Looney Tunes with the yawn of the century, I think it would be only fair if"—he paused, turning to lock eyes with Mindy—"if you would do me a favor and go get my hair."

Mindy didn't move.

Mr. Finelli rubbed the top of his head. "Would you hurry, please? I feel a chill coming on."

Mindy looked at her teacher, and then at the hair on the bottom of the fish tank. "You're not serious?" she said.

Mr. Finelli rubbed faster. "Absolutely, I'm freezing."

"Oh, gross." Mindy groaned. She wasn't sure if she was more grossed out by the thought of sticking her arm in the fish tank or by the sight of the teacher rubbing his bald head.

Mr. Finelli stopped rubbing and calmly pointed to his hair in the fish tank. "If you would, Mindy. Please get it now."

"I have only two words to say." Mindy smirked.

"And what might those two words be?" Mr. Finelli asked.

"*No* and *way*."

"I like this game." Mr. Finelli clapped his hands. "Now it's my turn." He counted quickly on his fingers, then announced, "I have only twenty-five words to say."

Mr. Finelli waited for Mindy to respond. When she didn't say a word, he commented sweetly, "Boy, for your own game, you're not very good at this, are you?

"Okay, then," he went on. "I'll take your part. 'And what might those twenty-five words be, Mr. Finelli?' " he said in an exact imitation of Mindy.

"Glad you asked, Mindy." Now Mr. Finelli sounded like Mr. Finelli. "Those twenty-five words are: If you don't go get my hair right now, and smile happily while you're doing it, everyone here will stay

**10**

at their desks until you do. Oops," Mr. Finelli blushed. "I think that was twenty-six words. You win."

"No fair!"

"It's her fault!"

"We didn't do anything!"

The shouts came from around the classroom. Mindy simply folded her arms and snapped out the words "I . . . don't . . . care."

"Fine," Mr. Finelli snapped back. "Then I'm glad I brought my lunch." He pulled a large silver thermos and a big brown bag out from under this desk. "Oh, yes, a few more words. There will be no talking, chewing, laughing, playing, reading, writing, tapping, tickling, eating, walking, asking, yawning, sleeping, or deep-sea diving until Ms. Mindy gets my hair. That goes for everyone here, except me of course. I'm the teacher, and I can do whatever I want." Mr. Finelli stuck out his tongue at Mindy and poured himself a cup of coffee.

Mr. Finelli looked into his lunch bag. "Good." He smiled. "I'm glad I brought enough for dinner too. Hey, look." He pulled out two Hostess cupcakes. "There's even enough for breakfast."

Everyone watched as Mr. Finelli scarfed down a baloney and cheese sandwich, three stalks of celery, seven Oreo cookies, a big grab bag of Doritos, two carrot sticks, three Strawberry Newtons, a handful of

Ritz Bits, a hard-boiled egg, one slice of cold pepperoni pizza, some leftover roast beef, and a peach.

Patting his belly, Mr. Finelli said, "I'd better save the rest for later." He winked at the class. "A bit of self-control is always important." He burped. "Isn't that right, Mindy?"

All of the students stared at Mindy. Frankie's stomach growled.

Mindy just stared straight ahead.

Mr. Finelli glanced at the fish tank and back again.

Mindy sighed, rolled her eyes and thought three words: *for*, *get*, and *it*.

Mr. Finelli rolled his eyes back at her and unwrapped a peanut butter granola bar. He then pulled a copy of *Mad* magazine out of his briefcase and put his feet up on his desk. "Whenever you're ready," he said softly. "Whenever."

For a long while it seemed like "whenever" might never come. One hour became two. Two hours turned to three. If Mindy hadn't had plans to meet her cousin Amanda for a Slurpee right after school, she and her classmates might still be sitting at their desks, staring at Mr. Finelli's bald head.

As the final bell sounded, Mindy gave in. She slapped her hands down on her desk. Everyone jumped, particularly Frankie, who was very close to finding a way to sleep with his eyes wide open.

"Okay, you win!" Mindy scowled as she got up

and started walking toward the fish tank. When she passed Mr. Finelli, she sneered and said, "For now."

Mindy rolled up the right sleeve of her red flannel shirt. When she reached the fish tank, she held her nose, closed her eyes, and without hesitation plunged her arm into the slimy depths. She felt one goldfish touch her wrist as it swam by. Another gave her a quick little fishy kiss near the elbow.

It took a few moments of searching through the sand and pebbles to find the hair in the seaweed. Finally she yanked the tattered, tangled, and twisted toupee from the tank. Everyone cheered—including Mr. Finelli.

Mindy walked over to the teacher's desk and handed Mr. Finelli his dripping hair. It was one of the most humiliating moments in her life.

"Thank you." Mr. Finelli took the sopping-wet toupee from Mindy and immediately plopped it onto his head. As the green water trickled down his face, Mr. Finelli smiled and said, "Class dismissed."

# Chapter
# Three

**Mindy was miffed.** Mindy was muttering. But most of all Mindy was *mad* when she and her new classmates walked down the deserted halls and out the school door. "If I get rabies or something from that stupid fish, Finelli-belly is going to be the first one I bite." Mindy rubbed her arm and looked around at Frankie, Jeff, Samantha, and the others. Jeff and Samantha nodded their approval. Frankie started to growl.

"You made me miss my lunch," he snapped. Frankie admired Mindy's guts for standing up to the teacher, but when it came right down to it, his own stomach was his number-one concern.

The class was split about fifty-fifty over what Mindy had done. Half wished she hadn't given in.

The other half wished she'd just gotten the dumb toupee in the first place so they wouldn't have had to sit there all day watching Mr. Finelli eat. Everyone, however, agreed with Mindy's next statement.

"We can't let him get away with it."

After a loud chorus of "yeahs," "yays," and "yahoos," Mindy knew these were her kind of people. "Okay. What do you all think about meeting tonight at the mall, say sevenish?"

"Sevenish," the sixth-graders echoed.

All of the students giggled, except for Mindy. Being kissed by a fish always made her a bit cranky. She got right to the heart of the matter. "We have to get back at that teacher for what he did to me," she said solemnly. Mindy looked from student to student, making eye contact with each one. "Or next time he may do it to you."

A few of the others in the class rubbed their arms, as if imagining what the slimy fish-tank water would feel like. Mindy knew that she'd made her point. "I say we meet at the arcade."

"Nah," Frankie said. "Burger King."

"Cool." Mindy smiled. "This is going to be fun."

Everyone, except Mindy, headed off toward their homes. Mindy set course for the 7-Eleven store, where she and her cousin Amanda were thrown out for sucking grape Slurpee stuff right out of the spigot. Mindy started to explain to the store manager that she felt paper cups were bad for the environment. Unfortunately he didn't seem very interested in protecting the earth at that particular moment.

Because it was a school night, only about a third of the class made it to the mall. Of those who did show, most had to leave early or were with their parents. It was quickly decided that Mindy, Jeff, Frankie, and Samantha would be on the Action to Reject Finelli Committee, or ARF. (The *to* was silent.) The four of them plainly had the most experience in making teachers regret ever having picked up a piece of chalk.

As they swapped stories about torturing teachers, Mindy couldn't help feeling impressed. Frankie had once driven a teacher so crazy, she quit to become a deep-sea shark photographer because she wanted a safer way to make a living. And Samantha had managed to convince her old principal that his office was haunted by the ghosts of a dog named Pumpernickel and a turtle named Lampshade. Jeff had once tricked the school cook into eating his own meatloaf and lima bean lunch. The cook almost died, and Jeff's parents were called in for a conference.

Now this fearsome foursome had been chosen to come up with a plan to reduce their teacher to jelly.

"Grape jelly," Frankie added. "I really like grape jelly."

• • •

Soon after the committee was formed, most of the students had to go home. This left the four ARF members alone in front of Burger King. Frankie suggested their first course of action: "Let's eat!"

After ordering hamburgers, small Cokes, and large fries, they settled into a booth. "That Mr. Fin-yelley is a one-hundred-percent creep," Mindy said.

"Like, a total nar," Samantha agreed.

"Did you see him eat?" Jeff groaned. "It made me sick."

"It made me hungry." Frankie stuffed a fistful of fries into his mouth. Like the others, Frankie had never met a teacher he didn't dislike. Mr. Finelli was certainly no exception. But while he would never say it out loud, Frankie had to admit that the man sure knew how to pack a lunch.

Samantha watched Frankie chew. His mouth was half open, so there could be no doubt about what he was eating. "Yeech," Samantha said. "Don't you like to do anything but eat?"

"Yeah," Frankie answered. "Now that you mention it . . . I also like to hit."

"Here, have my fries." Samantha quickly pushed her fries in front of Frankie. "A growing boy like you needs his nourishment, don't-cha know?" she added, trying to sound just like her mother.

Jeff and Mindy laughed. Frankie took the fries. He looked at Samantha very seriously. He squinted his

**17**

eyes and spoke very slowly. "There's just one thing I got to know. And I got to know it right now."

"What is it?" Samantha sounded a little nervous.

"You want your pickle?"

"Red alert! Red alert! Red alert!" Jeff frantically whispered. He and Frankie were sitting on the side of the booth that faced the door. As Frankie looked up, he almost choked on Samantha's pickle.

Both girls turned and looked. Even in their worst nightmares no one could have predicted this. Mr. Finelli was walking into the restaurant and heading straight for the counter.

The four committee members sank down slowly into the booth as Mr. Finelli tried to decide between a cheeseburger and a chef salad. "What the chili dog," he said happily. "I'll take both." Mr. Finelli's voice practically boomed throughout the restaurant.

By this time Frankie, Mindy, Samantha, and Jeff had slid off the seats and onto the floor under the table. They heard Mr. Finelli ask the person behind the counter, "So, which chicken sandwich do you recommend?"

"Do you think he saw us?" Samantha whispered.

"Nah," Mindy said. "He only has eyes for food."

"What an oinker." Jeff giggled.

"But he's so skinny," Samantha pointed out.

"Okay, so he's a skinny oinker," Jeff acknowledged. "Look at all the food he's getting. I bet he grades papers with a red *pig* pen."

While Jeff, Mindy, and Samantha whispered oinking noises, Frankie was silent. His secret admiration for Mr. Finelli was growing with each menu item the teacher ordered. He'd never seen anyone, other than himself, with such an incredible ability to eat. In spite of himself Frankie was starting to wonder if he and Mr. Finelli were somehow related.

Abruptly the oinking came to a squealing halt. From under the table the four sixth-graders saw two brown pant legs alongside their booth. There was a Reebok hiking boot at the end of each leg. "Let's see, where should I sit?" they heard a familiar voice ask.

Mindy leaned into Frankie. Samantha pressed against Mindy. And Jeff tried to shove the whole group into the wall.

*Please pick someplace else. Please pick someplace else,* they all silently pleaded.

Sure enough, their plea was soon answered. But unfortunately for them the answer was no.

"I think I'll just sit right here in this booth," Mr. Finelli said. "I could use the leg room."

A tray clanked down on the tabletop. Then two legs bent. Next, to the total terror of those below, Mr. Finelli slid into the booth.

When it came to fast food, Mr. Finelli was one slow eater. He savored every bite of his burger and he popped the french fries into his mouth one by one. As he ate he kept crossing and uncrossing his legs, which kept those down under dodging and ducking from left to right and back again.

"We should have run when we had a chance," Samantha whispered.

"When did we have a chance?" Mindy whispered back.

Samantha thought for a second, then said, "Before we got here."

Mr. Finelli hummed while he ate. He read the newspaper from cover to cover. He tapped his fingers continuously on the tabletop, which after fifteen minutes began to drive Jeff and Frankie to the brink of going bonkers.

But no one was prepared for what happened next. As he dug into his chef salad, Mr. Finelli took off his right shoe.

All four people under the booth almost fainted. Mindy was hit the hardest. Mr. Finelli's foot was only about an inch and a half from her nose. His big toe stuck out through a hole in his sock. It seemed to be pointing at her. It was the biggest big toe Mindy had ever seen.

An hour slowly passed. With a satisfied pat of his stomach, Mr. Finelli finally finished his feast and slipped his shoe back on. He started to move out of the booth, and Mindy started to breathe again. Mr.

Finelli was leaving, and the ARF Committee hadn't been caught. Samantha and Frankie smiled. Jeff moved his fist up and down and mouthed silently, "Yes! Yes! Yes!"

"We made it." Mindy almost giggled out loud.

Then Mr. Finelli dropped his napkin.

Four pairs of eyes popped wide open and four chins dropped. Mr. Finelli's hand reached under the table. He started searching around for the napkin. His fingers came within a walrus whisker of Jeff's arm. They actually brushed against Samantha's sneakers.

Ever so carefully Mindy pushed the mustard-stained napkin over to where the hand was patting the floor. She had to do something; Mr. Finelli's index finger was less than an inch from Frankie's belly and closing in fast.

The hand touched the napkin, pulled away a bit, and then went back and touched it again. After a moment of checking to make sure the object was truly the napkin, the fingers formed the "okay" sign and flashed it all around.

The four sixth-graders watched as Mr. Finelli pulled the napkin out from under the table. Not two seconds later his hand returned. This time there was writing on his palm. In bold red letters were the words "Thanks. See you all in class tomorrow."

# Chapter Four

After escaping the mall the ARF Committee members ran to a nearby grocery store, where they played with the vegetables, calmed their nerves, and came up with a plan. Their strategy was based on a comment Frankie made while trying to juggle two cantaloupes. "Just because he tries to teach us doesn't mean we gotta learn."

Mindy instantly ran up and gave Frankie a quick kiss on his cheek, causing him to drop his cantaloupes. "You're brilliant!" she said. "Absolutely brilliant."

While wiping off the kiss, Frankie tried to think of some other "brilliant" thing to say, but the only thing that came to mind was "Reese's peanut butter cups."

Mindy took the lead. "Okay, here's what we do. Tomorrow, after Mr. Finelli-face takes attendance, no one says a word—not a peep." Mindy remembered that Mr. Finelli did not allow gum chewing in his classroom. "We'll just chew gum and blow bubbles. When I nod my head, everyone start chewing."

"But what about Mr. Finelli?" Jeff asked.

"Let him do whatever he wants to do. If he asks questions, we don't have to answer. If he tries to teach, like Frankie said, we don't gotta learn."

"Yeah, I guess that was kinda brilliant of me," Frankie said, hoping for another kiss.

But Mindy had already moved down the aisle to play with the zucchini.

The next day everyone in Mr. Finelli's class, except Frankie and Jeff, made it to school on time. Even Mindy was there, despite her best efforts to convince her parents that she was sick. They just didn't buy the sore-throat bit, didn't believe the stomachache routine, and didn't budge when Mindy begged to stay home because of bladder-control problems. All her mom said was, "You're giving *me* a headache. Get up and get ready for school. *NOW!*"

When Mr. Finelli called out Mindy's name at roll that morning, she sneered a quick "here" and prayed for a miracle that would instantly turn the clock to 3:15 P.M. and sound the escape bell. It also wouldn't hurt her feelings if the miracle included turning Mr.

Finelli into a little blue troll with bright pink hair, wearing a ballerina's outfit and army boots.

Mindy smiled while plotting her miracle. Mr. Finelli smiled back at her. Mindy thought, *If only you knew what I was thinking, you troll of a teacher.* Mr. Finelli winked and nodded. Surprised, Mindy quickly looked down and pretended to read her math book.

Just as Mindy looked down, the door flew open and in strolled Frankie and Jeff.

"Tardy-hardy, dude," Frankie said as he passed in front of Mr. Finelli's desk.

"Why are you two scholars so late?" Mr. Finelli asked. "Car trouble? Or did you and your wives have an argument over breakfast?"

"We ain't married," Frankie replied. The class laughed until Frankie turned around and glared at them with his fists clenched.

"*Aren't* married," Mr. Finelli corrected him. "And, I must say it's a good thing you're not. With grammar like that you'd probably go up to the altar and say 'I does.'"

Frankie looked confused. "So what's your point?"

Jeff decided to come to the rescue of his friend. "Keep your hair on, Mr. F. So we're a little late. As my dear old granny used to say, 'Better late than never.'"

"Keep coming late to my class, and *never* getting out of sixth grade will become a real possibility." Mr.

Finelli walked out from behind his desk and leaned back against the front. "Now, unless any of you would like to have a hair-raising, fish-filled adventure like Mindy's, I suggest we all do our jobs. I know"—Mr. Finelli snapped his fingers—"I'll teach and you'll learn. What a concept!"

At the mention of her name Mindy was jerked back to reality. She'd been staring at a poster on the wall to the right of the door. It was a photograph of a big full moon. The picture had been taken looking up through the leafless branches of a tree. In white letters were the words: "Happy are those who dream dreams . . . and are willing to pay the price to have them come true."

*How totally sap city*, Mindy thought. Still, she had stared at it for several minutes.

Actually all of the walls in Mr. Finelli's classroom were covered with posters, pictures, signs, and maps. Without a doubt it was one of the most unusual decorating jobs Mindy had ever seen.

Above the blackboard at the front of the room were the words WELCOME TO THE TWILIGHT ZONE in big blue letters. There was a one-way road sign that pointed up and a THIS SIDE UP sign pointing down. A mirror was hung above the words FIND YOURSELF. There were also DO NOT DISTURB, EXIT, BEWARE OF THE DOG, OUT TO LUNCH, CONSTRUCTION ZONE, YARD SALE, and NO PARKING signs everywhere.

In the far corner a skeleton hung from the ceiling. A name tag reading Max was stuck to its ribs. A sign that simply said FORMER STUDENT hung from a chain around its neck. Today old Max was wearing a Burger King crown and held a french fry between his clenched teeth.

Wherever Mindy looked she saw something that indicated that this was no ordinary classroom. Above the clock was a picture of an elephant, saying "Time's passing. Are you?" At the back of the room was a poster featuring the profiles of two hippos. They were nose to nose, and the caption read "After all is said and done, there's usually more said than done."

Mindy turned back toward Mr. Finelli and glared at him. Once it had become clear that her parents wouldn't let her stay home, Mindy had dressed quickly and been one of the first kids at school.

She'd told the rest of her class about the ARF Committee's plan before the first bell rang. As soon as Mr. Finelli closed his attendance book, Mindy nodded. She could barely contain her glee as each student pulled a piece of bubble gum out of a pocket, folder, or book bag and popped it into his or her mouth. The Battle of the Bubble had begun.

Without blinking an eye Mr. Finelli stepped back behind his desk and removed a piece of grape bubble gum. He held it high in the air over his head, carefully unwrapped it, tilted his face up, and dropped it into his mouth. Then he repeated the process. When he finally chomped down, his teeth dug into two pieces of gum. He looked at the class with a "Beat that, Bozos" look on his face.

Mindy smiled, tossed back her hair, and slowly raised three fingers into the air. Every student reached down and pulled up three pieces of gum. After a quick unwrapping ceremony the students now outgummed their teacher four to two.

Mr. Finelli found three more pieces of gum. The students, two. Mr. Finelli, four more. The students, three. Both sides now had nine pieces of bubble gum in their mouths. It was becoming quite clear that the entire class had bitten off more than it could chew.

Frankie started Phase Two of the Bubble Battle by blowing a medium-size bubble. The other students quickly did the same. After about ten seconds Frankie raised his right hand and snapped his fingers. A split second later everyone burst their bubbles.

The sound of snapping bubble gum exploded through the room. The sound was so loud that a glass bottle cracked and two posters fell from the walls.

The class stuffed the gum back in their mouths, confident of victory. But Mr. Finelli had not yet surrendered. Mindy watched in amazement as the teacher's cheeks puffed out and his lips puckered. Then a bubble began to appear, growing to twice the size of the ones they'd blown. Every student in the room jumped at the sound of the snap.

Jeff was the first to answer the challenge. He blew until his bubble topped Mr. Finelli's by a third. Everyone followed Jeff's lead.

Now facing Mr. Finelli was a classroom of students with volleyball-size bubbles sticking out from their lips. This time Jeff was the one to snap his fingers. Mr. Finelli covered his ears just in time. The sound waves were so powerful that the room seemed to shake. Max the skeleton rattled so hard that one of his rib bones fell to the floor. Two substitute teachers walking in the hall heard the explosions and went home, figuring the Fourth of July had come early.

"Not bad." Mr. Finelli always appreciated a well-blown bubble. "But beat this."

Mr. Finelli started to blow and didn't stop until his bubble reached basketball proportions. From Mindy's desk it looked as if Mr. Finelli's face had been replaced by a round, pink-purple ball.

Mindy giggled. "Hey, Mr. Finelli," she mumbled through a mouthful of gum. "I've had bubble-head teachers before, but—"

Mindy didn't have the chance to finish her statement. Mr. Finelli snapped the bubble back into his mouth. He did it with such force that it might have been picked up on some earthquake scientist's seismograph machine.

Mindy looked at Frankie. Frankie looked at Mindy. No one had to say a word. They knew it was time for their bubbles to go ballistic. Both started banging slowly on their desks with one hand. Everyone did the same. Both reached for yet another piece of gum. Everyone followed suit.

The whole class chewed to the beat they were pounding out. The wad of gum in each mouth now totaled ten pieces. Their jaws hurt, their teeth ached, but on they chewed. This was going to be the bubble to end all bubbles.

Like a big bad wolf in search of a ham sandwich, the students started to huff and puff and blow their bubbles out. The bubbling crew blew and blew. Their bubbles grew and grew. They grew past the size of Ping-Pong balls, red rubber balls, and hard balls. They grew bigger and rounder than softballs and volleyballs.

When they matched Mr. Finelli's basketball-size bubble, they kept right on growing. The incredible growth spurt didn't stop until Mr. Finelli faced a sea of beach-ball-size bubbles.

Even though Mindy couldn't see her desk because her bubble was in the way, she managed to grab hold of a pen and rip a sheet of paper out of a notebook. Reaching around her bubble, she wrote down a few words and pushed the paper toward Mr. Finelli.

She watched the teacher pick up the note and read its message: "What are you going to do now, Mr. Loser-elli?"

Mr. Finelli yawned, then abruptly snapped his fingers. Thinking that Frankie had given the signal, everyone in the class but Frankie sucked back and snapped their bubbles. Even Mindy followed the cue, without realizing what had happened. Finally, not wanting to be left alone holding the bubble, Frankie did the same.

Now, with small or medium bubbles, snapping is rarely a problem. Most people can handle large bubbles. Even super-size bubbles can often be snapped with the snapper's ending up with little more than gum-coated lips. But bubbles of the size the class had blown on this day were an entirely different matter.

Mr. Finelli's class quickly realized they'd just made one buffo of a bubble blunder.

Mindy saw a pink, gooey wall racing toward her face at an incredible speed. Samantha felt the first hit of gick stick to her hair, nose, and chin. Jeff found himself instantly coated from forehead to flannel shirt with bananaberry Hubba Bubba. Frankie tried to duck, but his gum was quicker than his head.

Where once-proud bubbles had ruled supreme, now sat only students—their hair and heads, faces and fronts covered with gluey, gummy guck.

Mr. Finelli looked at Mindy, threw his arms up in the air, and said, "Okay, you win."

Before anyone could pry their lips apart to respond, there was a knock at the classroom door. Mr. Finelli walked out into the hall. About thirty seconds later he came back in, beaming from ear to ear.

"Great news!" he said excitedly. "We won the drawing!"

"What drawing?" Samantha mumbled, her lips still half stuck together.

"The drawing for which sixth-grade class will represent Doverton in the district-wide essay contest."

Every year the school district held an essay contest. Each school drew the room number of one of its sixth-grade classes out of a hat. The winners had to come up with an essay on a given subject, and several students from each class would then read part of the essay at a special assembly. A panel of judges picked the winner. The class finishing first would get a pizza party, and each student would get a plaque.

Everyone groaned through their gum.

"Big whoop." Mindy had cleared most of the gum away from her mouth.

"And"—Mr. Finelli clapped his hands—"this year the contest is going to be on TV."

"Super-big whoop." Mindy twirled a gum-coated index finger in the air.

By this time Mr. Finelli was practically jumping up and down. "Wait until you hear the topic for the essays. Are you ready for this? It's 'What we like about our teacher.' "

Mindy smiled. In fact Mindy started to laugh.

# Chapter Five

"**We'll be able** to embarrass that teacher creature on TV in front of the whole world!" Mindy could barely contain her excitement as she spoke with Frankie over the phone later that evening. "And then we'll . . . OUCH! Mom, be careful! OOOOOOUUUUUCCCCCHHHHHH!"

Frankie dropped the phone and held his ringing ear. Mindy's mom was still trying to get all the gum out of her daughter's hair.

Frankie, on the other hand, wasn't at all worried about the gum in his hair because he no longer had any—hair, that is. After one look at her son, Frankie's mom had marched him straight to the barbershop.

The barber had thought the sight of Frankie's hair coated with gummy glop was one of the funniest things he'd ever seen. In fact once the joker had finally stopped laughing, he announced in a very serious voice, "I think we can save the head. But the hair will have to come out."

"Frankie? Frankie!" Frankie heard Mindy's voice coming from the telephone receiver on the floor.

"Sorry, Mind." He picked up the phone. "But I think your last ouch broke my ear."

"Well, use the other one."

Frankie shifted the receiver to his left ear just in time to hear "OUCH! You're pulling out my hair! STOP! STOP! OOOOUUUUCCCCCHHHHH!" Frankie dropped the phone and ran out of the house.

After screaming in vain for Frankie and then being told by her mom to watch her language, Mindy hung up and called Samantha.

Samantha's mom had used peanut butter (creamy) to get the gum out of her daughter's hair. It seemed to help, but it left Samantha smelling like a jar of Jif.

"It's perfect," Mindy told her fellow ARF Committee member. "With this essay contest we'll be able to move our Action to Reject Finelli into prime time."

Samantha was just as excited about the contest as Mindy. "You're right. I can't wait to see his face when we go on TV and tell everyone that our teacher is a jerk."

"*Jerk* is a good word," Mindy said. "But I think *creep* would be a little better."

"How about *weenie?*" Samantha giggled.

"*Wacko?*" Mindy giggled back.

"Or *wuss*," Samantha suggested.

"Or *weirdo.*"

"I say *dork.*"

"*Dip?*"

"*Dragon head?*"

"*Fish face?*"

"*Beetle butt?*"

The two girls were on a roll. They didn't stop until Mindy said, "*Buffalo barf burger brain?*" and Samantha almost got sick.

"Seriously," Samantha said, "we've got to make this essay really great."

"I know." Mindy knew she sounded a little angry and disappointed, but she didn't care. She had been serious about *buffalo barf burger brain*. She liked it way better than *beetle butt*.

Samantha tried to get Mindy's mind off the subject of bison bellyaches. "When is that assembly, anyway?"

"Two weeks from tomorrow, I think," Mindy said sadly. "But I don't know. I'm just not into it anymore." She sniffled.

"Look," Samantha said impatiently. "We can use what you said, you know, the buffalo stuff, okay?"

"Okay!" Mindy was back into it. "The important

thing is," she went on happily, "Mr. Finnuffalo can't find out what we're going to do."

"I know," Samantha said. "We'll have to pretend to be good students."

"Nah," Mindy replied. "He'd never believe it. He might be a jerk . . . but he ain't a idiot."

"*Isn't an* idiot," Samantha corrected. "You don't *got* to be so dumb."

Mindy sighed. "From the sound of things I think we've both been hanging with Frankie way too long, and we've only known him for two days."

"Frankie's been hanging with Frankie way too long." Samantha laughed. "He's known himself almost his whole life."

Mindy was silent. For some reason she didn't like anyone except herself saying anything bad about Frankie. After a long pause she finally said, "We'd better get busy and do our homework."

"Homework?" Samantha sounded shocked. "You're actually going to do homework?"

"Yeah. We have to plan out two full weeks of teacher tortures."

"Phew." Samantha was relieved. "You scared me for a second there."

After tossing a few ideas back and forth Mindy and Samantha decided that they should meet Jeff and Frankie the next day before school, to finalize their plans.

Samantha called Jeff. She had to shout at the top of her lungs into the phone for him to hear her over the two blow dryers he was using to heat his head. His parents had made him stick his head into a bag filled with ice so that they could get the gum out of his hair.

"Sh-sh-sh-sure. I-I-I-I'll b-b-b-be th-th-th-there," Jeff said between chattering teeth.

"Cool," Samantha giggled. "Make that *ice* cool."

"V-v-v-very f-f-f-funny!" Jeff hung up the phone.

Meanwhile Mindy tried calling Frankie back. This time she had to leave a message because his mom said he was busy polishing his head.

# Chapter Six

**The ARF Committee** had decided to meet the next morning on the climbing thing that sat on the playground at school. It was made of logs and old tires. The PTA had bought it with the money they'd raised from the bake sale at open house. Nobody really knew what the thing was, but it was fun to climb on and fall from.

Jimmy Shulin was the only one who didn't like it. Frankie didn't understand that one bit. "Just because he fell off and broke his arm in two places, he's gotta make a big stink about it?"

This morning, when Mindy and Samantha came around the corner of the school, they saw that Jeff and Frankie were already on top of the climbing thing—trying to push each other off. Frankie won. Jeff hit the ground—bottom first.

Mindy and Samantha ran up to their fallen friend. They each grabbed an arm and pulled Jeff to his feet. "Are you okay?" Samantha asked.

"Really, are you all right?" Mindy asked.

Jeff was glad that they hadn't said what his parents would have said: "Only your pride is hurt." In this case pride was the least of Jeff's concerns. Right now the source of his pain was lower and around back, and he wished he could rub what needed rubbing most. Instead he just nodded, mumbled "yeah," and started to rub his arm.

Then Frankie shouted, "Hey, maybe his butt's busted. We'd better put it in a cast." He was laughing so hard, he almost fell from the climbing thing.

"Shut up!" Jeff shouted.

"Yeah," Samantha agreed. "Leave him alone."

"Me, king of the mountain." Frankie started pounding on his chest like Tarzan.

"You, jerk of the jungle," Mindy said.

"By the way, great haircut," Samantha commented sweetly.

"Thanks," Frankie said, trying to hide his surprise at her tone. "You really think it looks good?"

Samantha smiled. "Yeah, on a bowling ball." She turned away.

When Frankie saw that both girls were paying more attention to Jeff, he quickly climbed down and patted Jeff on the back. "Sorry, man. It was an accident."

Jeff, Mindy, and Samantha looked at each other, and said, "So's this." All three pushed Frankie. He fell back, tripped over a log, and found himself bottom down in a puddle of water left over from last night's thunderstorm.

Frankie felt the water soaking through his jeans. He also heard his friends laughing. "That ain't funny," Frankie cried. "I didn't push him into no water. That's cheating!"

"Come on, Mr. Soppy Pants." Mindy helped Frankie up. "We have work to do."

Mindy and Samantha sat down on logs and pulled out notebooks so they could write down their plans. Frankie and Jeff both said that they preferred to stand.

"Okay." Mindy called the ARF Committee meeting to order. "We've agreed that we'll use the essay contest to get back at Mr. Foolelli big-time. Until then we have to make sure he thinks it's business as usual. Any ideas?"

Frankie was the first to speak. "I brought a few things." He pulled a large paper bag from an army knapsack that was supposed to be for his books. The bag was marked "Basic Assault Kit." In small print Frankie had written the words "Keep out of reach of parents."

"Let's see what you have," Samantha said.

"Okay," Frankie replied. "It ain't much, but it'll get us started." He turned over the bag, and out tumbled a whoopee cushion, a can of tapioca pudding, some fake doggie-do, and a sour dill pickle. Frankie shook the bag. A can of whipped cream hit the ground, followed by several red paint balls, a jar of chunky spaghetti sauce, and a yellow squeeze container of mustard.

"Is that it?" Mindy asked sarcastically.

Frankie tapped the bottom of the bag with his hand. Out came a tube of glue, three bottles of food coloring, and twenty-seven boxes of exploding poppers. Frankie looked into the bag. "That's it."

"Why the pickle?" Samantha asked.

"Oh, yeah," Frankie picked up the pickle and took a big bite. "Ahh," he sighed. "Breakfast . . . the most important meal of the day."


The ARF Committee members met their classmates outside the school building before the last bell rang that morning. The last thing any one of them wanted to be was tardy.

Mindy quickly explained to the others that they'd use the essay contest to embarrass the Fritos out of Finelli, and Frankie handed out the boxes of poppers.

"Whenever Finelli isn't looking," Frankie commanded, "step on one of these. It'll drive him pistach-ios. Then leave the rest of this stuff to us."

"Yeah," Mindy agreed. "Remember, we can't let him know about the essay plan. In fact . . ." Mindy reached over and grabbed two kids. "I have a job for you two." Mindy put her arms around her startled classmates and pulled them close. Both of the people she'd picked were pretty good students and moderately well behaved. They'd landed in Mr. Finelli's class because of an awful case of bad luck. Compared with the rest of the class they looked like geniuses and saints.

Mindy looked to her left and to her right. "Yeah, you two will do nicely."

"Do what nicely?" one of them asked.

"You two are going to volunteer to write the essay. That will really put him off the track."

"I'm too busy to write the essay," the other kid said. "Besides, I have a paper . . ."

Mindy stuffed the boy's own hand into his mouth. "You're not going to really write it, creep meat. You're only going to say you are. The four of us"—Mindy pointed to Samantha, Jeff, and Frankie—"are going to do the real writing. And we'll also read the essay on TV, okay?"

"Okay," the boy mumbled through his hand as the rest of the class applauded the plan.

• • •

Meanwhile, Mindy soon found out that Mr. Finelli had a plan of his own. He called in sick.

"What a rip-off!" Frankie growled.

"No flippin' fair!" Samantha shouted.

"He's got to be kidding!" Jeff stormed around the room.

"Boy, he's good," Mindy whispered. "He's really good."

When everyone walked into the classroom that morning, their teacher target was nowhere in sight. But his presence could definitely still be felt.

There was a small package wrapped in plain brown paper on each desk. A long message, written in orange chalk, covered the blackboard. It read,

Dear Students (You, too, Frankie),

I, Mr. Floyd Raymond Ronald Finelli the First, being of sound mind and body (not counting the little bulge over my belt), do hereby hand out today's assignments. Since I am obviously not here, and don't intend to be, you are on your own. I was going to arrange for a substitute, but I thought that would be too cruel. Some of my best friends are subs, and I am not a cruel man.

"Some of my best friends are subs too," Frankie said.

"What subs are those?" Jeff scoffed.

"Meatball subs, steak subs, ham-and-cheese subs."

Frankie rubbed his belly. "Yeah . . ." He got a dreamy look in his eyes. "Some of my best friends are subs."

"Be quiet, foodasaurus," Mindy said. "I'm trying to read."

In light of the fact that there is no one here to teach you something new, I thought it would be interesting to see how much you already know.

"This is looking really snaky," Jeff said.

"So's your sister." Frankie laughed.

"Shut up. Don't talk about Fang that way." Jeff made a hissing sound, fell to the floor, and tried to bite Frankie's ankle.

"Would someone please step on him?" Samantha concentrated on the next line in the note: I'm sure you've all noticed the little gifts I left on your desks. Can you guess what they are?

Everyone looked at the brown-paper-covered bundles. They were about eight inches wide, ten inches long, and a half inch thick.

Come on. Somebody guess, the note continued.

"TV dinners?" Frankie said out loud.

"You're talking to a stupid note on the blackboard, dorkus," Mindy snorted. She stopped mid-snort when she read the next line.

**No, Frankie, sorry. They aren't TV dinners. But it was a good guess. Let me give you a little hint. They're tests. Did anybody guess tests?**

In spite of themselves half the class found themselves shaking their heads no.

**No one guessed tests? Bummer. You would have won an all-expense paid trip to Toys "R" Us, where you would have been given a shopping cart and three minutes to fill it with all the toys you could grab. But don't worry, all is not lost. You do win the second-place prize. You get to take the test.**

Mindy threw her package down onto the floor, stepped on it, and slapped high fives with Jeff.

Samantha was laughing. "Oh, yeah," she said. "Like, we're going to listen with no teacher here? Uh-huh, *rrrright.*" Samantha rolled her eyes. The next line in the note made her mouth drop wide open.

**Stop rolling your eyes as you always do, Samantha. Your face might freeze that way one day. Every one of you will take this test for two very good reasons. First of all, it counts for 50—no, make that 52 percent of your final grade.**
**Second, if even one person fails . . . you all fail. So unless you've selected sixth grade as your career, I suggest you get started. Oh, and Mindy, I do think it would be wise**

for you to pick your test up off the floor. I hope it isn't too
badly damaged.

Everyone slowly started to unwrap their packages
as they continued to read the note. Mindy picked hers
up off the floor and tried to wipe away her footprint.

This test is made up of 500 questions, 32 pages, 17
sections, 1,176 sentences, and a blank doodle page for anyone
who finishes early. There are no rules. Therefore no matter
how hard you might try, it's impossible to cheat. So, without
any additional delay, students, grab your pencils and sharpen
your wits. On your mark. Get set. Go—to the store for a loaf
of bread! HA HA. Just kidding. GO!
    P.S. If you have time, why not start on the essay for the
contest. I'm sure there are a lot of nice things you'd like to
say about me right now.

"Do they allow swear words in the essay contest?"
Frankie grumbled. "I have a couple that would fit Mr.
Finelli just fine."

"Like what?" Jeff asked.

"Like—"

Mindy put her hand over Frankie's mouth. "Not
now, slime mouth. We have a test to take."

"We what?" everyone asked, turning to Mindy in
absolute shock.

"You mean we're actually going to do what *he* says?" Jeff pointed toward Mr. Finelli's desk.

Mindy took her hand away from Frankie's mouth and wiped it off on his shirt. "Yeah." She smiled a sneaky smile.

"But why?" Frankie frowned a confused frown.

"Because he doesn't think we will," Mindy answered.

Frankie looked more confused than ever.

Samantha tried to help. "You see, Frankie," she said to him as if he were a two-year-old. He didn't like it, but that didn't stop her. "What Mindy is saying is that if we do what Mr. Finelli says, then we won't be doing what he really wants us to do."

Frankie nodded his head. "Ain't that just like a grown-up." He had no idea what Samantha was talking about, but he sure wasn't going to ask any more questions.

In order to embarrass him further, Samantha was about to ask Frankie to explain the plan to the whole class, but Mindy stepped in, to save his day. "Mr. Fink-nelli expects us *not* to take the test. He expects us to fail. I say we really freak out the old buzzard and all get an A."

"There's no way," Jeff said. "I didn't even get an A in kindergarten."

"Yeah," Frankie agreed. "And anyway, how are we gonna have time to answer five hundred questions?"

**47**

"He said no rules, so we can use our books." Mindy walked up in front of the class. "So we will." She looked around the room. "Who brought a book?"

Nobody said a word.

"Come on. Somebody must have brought a book. I mean, this is school, right?"

Slowly and reluctantly five of Mindy's classmates raised their hands.

"Cool." Mindy smiled. "Here's what we do. Let's break up into five groups. Each group will only have to answer one hundred questions, and then we'll share the answers. That way no one will have too much to do in one day. What do you guys think?"

After a brief pause Frankie stood up and said, "Mindy, don't take this wrong, but I think you're a genius."

"Hey, I didn't get to sixth grade on my looks." Mindy tossed her hair to one side. "Although I could have."

For the rest of the day the five groups found and shared answers. By the time the final bell rang, all five hundred questions had been answered, and the tests had been piled neatly on Mr. Finelli's desk.

Mindy stood on a chair and led the class cheer:

*We're cool . . . we know it.*
*We're cool . . . we show it.*

*Try and beat us . . . there's no way.*
*Listen up to what we say.*
*We're cool . . . we know it.*
*We're cool . . . we show it.*

After a round of low, medium, and high fives, the bell rang and everyone started to file out of the room. Half the class was laughing, the other half shouting happily about what they'd just accomplished.

"I bet Mr. Finelli isn't ready for this," Samantha said proudly.

"Yeah," Mindy agreed. "He probably never had a class of all-A students before."

Mindy and Samantha bumped hips three times, spun around in a circle, and walked out the door.

Frankie and Jeff were the last to leave. Frankie had planned it that way. When they were alone, he walked up to Mr. Finelli's desk. He pulled the can of whipped cream from his knapsack, shook it, opened the top desk drawer and quickly filled it to the top with Reddi Wip.

"You're cool," Jeff cheered.

"I know it," Frankie answered.

# Chapter Seven

"**This is your lucky day,**" Mr. Finelli said as he greeted the class the next morning.

"Why?" Samantha yawned as she took her seat.

"Because . . . I'M BOCK." Mr. Finelli tried to sound like the Terminator. Unfortunately his voice cracked on the word *bock*, which made him sound more like a chicken. He quickly moved on to the next subject. "Unless someone objects, I think it's time for us to do some serious education-type business."

Without looking down, Mr. Finelli opened his top desk drawer and reached inside. The stench of stale whipped cream filled the air. Jeff had to bite his tongue to avoid laughing. Frankie felt his stomach start to jiggle with a giggle that didn't know the word *stop*.

Both boys expected their teacher to end up wrist deep in Reddi Wip. Instead he pulled yesterday's tests out of the drawer and plopped the completely dry stack of papers onto his desk with a loud "thunk."

Frankie and Jeff looked at each other with "What the heck happened?" expressions on their faces.

Mr. Finelli walked right up to them. "Frankie, Jeff, would you please get your workbooks out of your desks." Frankie and Jeff were still too surprised by what had happened to think about what might come next.

Numbly they lifted their desktops and reached in. Both boys screamed as they felt soft, wet, sticky goo cover their fingers and hands. They felt it ooze under their shirtsleeves before they yanked their arms out of their desks.

Blobs of whipped cream flew across the room as Jeff and Frankie tried to shake off the gucky glops that stuck beneath their nails and between their fingers. By this time everyone else in the class was either ducking or laughing. Suddenly both boys were hit with rolls of paper towels, thrown by a very smug-looking teacher.

Mr. Finelli touched his tongue and then his leg with one finger, making a hissing sound. "Whoa, I am hot today." He spun around in a circle. "I'm scorching!"

It took several minutes for order to be restored and for Jeff and Frankie to clean off. Once both tasks were accomplished, Mr. Finelli looked over the class and rested his hands on the pile of tests. "I guess you all proved my point. As I've always said, I don't care how you spell it, *studying* usually ends with an A."

"You mean we all got A's?" Mindy said innocently, batting her eyes. "Why . . . I just know you didn't think the young folks in this class could ever get all-A's."

"Shocked the shamrocks out of me," Mr. Finelli replied with a wink. "I mean, you all must have"—Mr. Finelli put his palms up to his cheeks and faked surprise—"opened books. Maybe, dare I say it, you . . . you . . . you read something."

Suddenly Mindy's satisfaction turned as sour as a lemon-and-vinegar milkshake left out in the sun on the hottest day of the year. "You tricked us," she shouted.

"No," Mr. Finelli answered. "I gave you a choice, and you chose to learn."

Mindy's face turned a shade of red that would make any radish proud. She kicked herself under her desk. *We did just what he wanted us to do*, she thought. *And I walked right into his trap.*

"And I understand that you, Mindy, organized the whole thing." Mr. Finelli was beaming. "Congratulations."

Mindy slumped down in her seat, trying to disappear.

"Who knows," Mr. Finelli continued, "maybe one day you'll become a great teacher."

Mindy almost fainted. It was bad enough to think that Mr. Finelli had fooled her. He didn't have to be insulting on top of it.

Mindy had always thought of teachers as the enemy. She sure didn't want to grow up to become her own worst nightmare.

"I mean, who knows what each of you will end up doing with your life." Mr. Finelli walked up to Samantha. "For example, take Samantha. Maybe she'll become a lawyer. After all, she likes to argue with people in authority."

"I do not!" Samantha folded her arms and stomped her feet under her desk.

"And Jeff." Mr. Finelli moved around the room. "You're always acting up. Maybe you'll be a great actor."

Jeff got up on his desk and started doing a scene from *Romeo and Juliet*.

" 'Romeo, Romeo, wherefore art thou, Romeo?' " he said in a falsetto. Then he dropped to the floor and spoke in his real voice. "I'm down in the bushes, Julie, the ladder broke."

Mr. Finelli went around the class, guessing what kind of work each student would do in the years ahead. The last person on the guess list was Frankie. "And Frankie . . . Frankie . . . Frankie . . ." Mr. Finelli was having a little trouble with this one. Finally he snapped his fingers. "I know. You're pretty much up in the air about everything. Maybe you'll be a jet pilot."

Frankie jumped up and spread his arms like airplane wings. Making a loud whooshing sound, he raced around the room. Everything was going along just fine until Frankie tried to make a turn at close to twice the speed of sound. His sneakers hit a slippery spot on the floor, and Jumbo Jet Frankie took off into the air. It was a short and rather tragic flight.

Frankie flew into the first row of students, who crashed into the second, who tumbled into the third. Mr. Finelli pulled Frankie up from the pile. "Maybe you're more suited to something more gentle—like professional wrestling."

Mr. Finelli helped the rest of the students off the floor. "The whole point is, you can go as far as your own special talent takes you, no matter what anyone says or thinks. I mean everyone has problems of one kind or another. Take Max here . . ."

Mr. Finelli walked over to Max the skeleton and lifted him off his stand. "You see, nobody ever thought Max could be a skeleton." He pulled up a chair, sat down, and placed Max on his lap like a ventriloquist's dummy. "People always said, 'You're too

**54**

fat to be a bag-o'-bones, Max. Be a butcher.' Isn't that right, Max?"

Mr. Finelli moved Max's jaw with one hand and held on to him from behind with the other.

"Yeah, guy," answered Max in a voice that sounded as smooth and sappy as a game-show host's. "It was no picnic becoming the skeleton I am today."

"What kind of problems did you face?" Mr. Finelli asked in his normal voice.

"I always took a lot of ribbing from my friends." Max's jaw went up and down. "Why, even my main man, Marty the Mannequin, said I was a bonehead to try it."

Several people in the class started to giggle. Everyone else, except Mindy, was smiling.

"That had to be tough." Mr. Finelli put Max's arm around his shoulders and turned the skeleton's head so that the two of them were talking eye to socket. "How did you handle all the criticism, Max?"

"Oh, I just let it tickle my funny bone."

"I didn't know it was so difficult to become a skeleton."

"I'm hip, man. A lot of my friends didn't make it."

"Why not?" Mr. Finelli asked.

"They didn't have the backbone."

Now most of the class was laughing.

"Is there anything I can do for you?" Mr. Finelli went on.

**55**

"As long as you're asking," the skeleton replied, "I'm really hungry. In fact I feel almost empty."

Mr. Finelli reached over to his desk and pulled a bag of Chee·tos out. He ripped it open and poured the contents into Max's mouth. The Chee·tos flew all over the floor.

In spite of herself Mindy found herself laughing along with the rest of the class. She had to admit that Mr. Finelli was pretty funny, even if he was a lousy ventriloquist. His lips moved every time he made Max speak.

"Ah," the skeleton/dummy said as the last Chee·to hit the floor. "I love those things, but they always make me thirsty."

"No problem, my friend." Mr. Finelli grabbed his thermos and filled a cup with steaming-hot coffee. He held it up to Max's open mouth.

"Don't!" Everyone in the class screamed, expecting the coffee to end up like the Chee·tos.

Without a word Mr. Finelli started to pour. Several students closed their eyes, while others watched and marveled as the coffee vanished as soon as it entered Max's mouth. Once the cup was empty, Max said, "Thanks, dude. I was bone dry."

This time nobody saw Mr. Finelli's mouth move.

Everybody gasped, except Mindy. "Chill out, turkeys," she said. "It's just a stupid magic trick. I saw a magician do that once on TV."

"Finelli the Fabulous, at your service." Mr. Finelli hung Max back up on his hook and took a large sweeping bow. Then he walked back to his desk. "I think what Max was trying to say is that each and every human being, no matter how successful, has stuff he or she has to overcome. Like George Washington. The man had wooden teeth, for splinters' sake. And that was way before Lemon Pledge was invented."

Mr. Finelli was getting really excited. He stuck one hand in his shirt at belly level and began marching up and down between rows of desks. He spoke with a French accent. "Even ze great Napoleon always held his stomach like zis." Mr. Finelli moaned and spoke in plain English. "I personally blame those 1812 tacos. But whatever the reason, it shows that even for the emperor of France, life was no bowl of french fries."

Frankie's stomach growled. Mindy yawned. She had found the magic tricks to be interesting, but all this talk about George Washington and Napoleon was putting her right to sleep.

Mr. Finelli laughed, walked up to Mindy, and said, "Keep awake, girl. I'm just getting warmed up."

Mindy yawned an even bigger yawn. She cut it short when Mr. Finelli peered into her mouth and said, "Hmmm, I think you have a cavity in a lower left molar. You know, I did take a mail-order dentistry course for a while. What say we drill for oil?"

Mindy's jaw slammed shut.

Mr. Finelli continued his lecture series on the Lifestyles of Famous People with Personal Problems. "Take Babe Ruth. He may have been the greatest baseball player ever. But could he get a candy bar named after him? Noooooo. What made things worse was that President Grover Cleveland's baby daughter, Ruth, could. Hence, Baby Ruth candy bars."

The teacher barely missed a beat before going on to his next subject. "Look at Tutankhamen, or King Tut, as his friends called him. He became pharaoh of Egypt when he was nine years old. But by the time he was eighteen . . . the boy was a mummy."

Mr. Finelli was starting to sweat. "Vincent van Gogh. What about Vincent van Gogh? He's one of the most famous artists in history. But when he was alive, he lopped off an ear. Do you want to know why? A lot of people think they know. But I think it was because during his whole life he sold only one, count 'em, *uno* painting. It's not that he was a slow worker or anything. In his last five years he painted eight hundred paintings.

"Then there's Albert Einstein. Talk about a bad-hair day. He had a bad-hair life. Even Superman has to deal with kryptonite. No one is free of obstacles in this life."

"Jeff has his sister," Frankie pointed out.

"Exactly," Mr. Finelli said. "The point is, so what

if people call you jerks, losers, toad brains, idiots, clowns, lunatics, mad hatters, goofballs, numb noggins, nincompoops, dolts, dullards, dunces, simpletons, saps, or just plain stupid."

"Hey!" Frankie sounded offended.

"Nothing personal," Mr. Finelli said.

"Oh, okay." Frankie sounded relieved.

"Remember, no matter what they say you can't do," Mr. Finelli continued, "it's what *you* say you *can* do that matters."

Mindy looked around the classroom. To her horror, all of her classmates—even Frankie—were absolutely rapt, listening to Mr. Finelli's lecture. What was more frightening was the fact that Mindy herself had been paying attention. She couldn't remember the last time she'd listened this closely in class. Thank goodness the bell rang, returning her to her senses.

As everyone got up to go to the lunchroom, Mindy whispered to all the kids around her, "I say we *can* drive this teacher permanently peanuts with our essay. What do you guys say?"

When nobody said a word, Mindy knew it was time for a little ARF Committee action. She had never dealt with a pro-teacher movement before, and she sure didn't intend to start dealing with one now.

# Chapter Eight

"**Did you hear** what he called us?" Mindy pulled the entire class aside on the playground right after school. "Did you hear it?"

Mindy looked at Samantha, who got the hint and climbed onto the first rung of the monkey bars. "Yeah," she said. "Like, losers? Lunatics? Toad brains?"

Samantha looked at Jeff. He had climbed up to the second rung. "Are we going to let him get away with it?" he shouted.

"No." Everyone sounded a little unsure of whether they meant what they were saying.

Mindy climbed to the very top. "He said, are we going to let that *teacher* get away with it?"

"No." This time there was more strength in the class's response.

"Are we going to make that Mr Jerk-elli wish he never heard of that old essay contest?" she screamed.

"Yes!"

"Are we going to let a teacher beat us?" Mindy was now shrieking.

"No!" Now everyone was shrieking right along with her.

"Are we going to order pizza?" Frankie cried.

Everyone looked at Frankie, who threw up his arms. "Just wondering," he said meekly.

"Look, we have less than two weeks to come up with an essay to finish Finelli once and for all," Mindy went on. "Any ideas?"

Nobody raised a hand or said a word.

Frankie looked at his classmates. He clenched his fists. "Someone better come up with something." Frankie was still thinking about pizza. "Let's wrap this up before I'm late for dinner."

Mindy just stared at him. Then suddenly she cried, "You're *brilliant!*" She raced up to Frankie and gave him a big kiss on the cheek.

"Yeech!" Frankie said, but he was smiling while he said it. For the second time Mindy had kissed him after he'd come up with an idea. *Gee,* he thought while gently touching his cheek, *this thinking stuff can really pay off. I'm going to have to start doing it on purpose.*

"What did he say that was so brilliant?" Jeff asked.

"Tell them, Frankie," Mindy said. "Say it again."

Now Frankie had to figure out exactly what it was he'd said. He took a shot at it. "You mean about the pizza?"

"No, silly." Mindy laughed. "I mean what you said about wrapping this thing up."

"Oh." Frankie paused, trying to figure out what was so great about worrying about missing dinner.

"You want us to wrap up Mr. Finelli?" Jeff sounded as confused as Frankie looked.

Mindy tapped her foot impatiently and looked toward the sky as if she were praying for help. "I don't want us to *wrap* him up. I want us to *rap* him down."

Jeff said what everyone was thinking. "Huh?

"You know, like . . ." Mindy started to clap her hands and snap her fingers in rhythm. *Clap-snap. Clap-snap. Clap-snap-clap.*

Then Mindy started her rap:

> "*Mis-ter Finelli . . .*
> *They say he can teach.*
> *But he smells like skunk*
> *And he looks like a leech.*"

Mindy kept clapping and snapping. "Like that," she said. "Come on, you guys, make up something."

Slowly other class members started to clap and

snap. Soon everybody was in time, and Jeff was center stage.

*Clap-snap. Clap-snap. Clap-snap-clap!*

> "*Mis-ter Finelli . . .*
>   *His hair is a wig.*
>   *His nose is like Pinocchio's . . .*
>   *He eats like a pig.*"

Samantha stepped forward.
*Clap-snap. Clap-snap. Clap-snap-clap!*

> "*He ain't no teacher.*
>   *He ain't so cool.*
>   *He's really half creature.*
>   *And the other half fool.*"

Everyone started to join in. The situation was getting "verse" by the second.
*Clap-snap. Clap-snap. Clap-snap-clap!*

> "*He pretends to be Napoleon.*
>   *He talks to bones named Max.*
>   *Our problems keep on rollin' in*
>   *With each dumb joke he cracks.*"

*Clap-snap. Clap-snap. Clap-snap-clap!*

*"He spends his nights with Dracula.*
*He spends his days with rats.*
*His favorite food is liver stew*
*Mixed with the spit of bats."*

"Yuck yuck yuck yuck yuck-yuck-yuck!" Mindy, Samantha, and three other girls rapped together.
*Clap-snap. Clap-snap. Clap-snap-clap!*

*"His name is Finelli.*
*He's mean and he's creepy.*
*He thinks his words are fine and sweet*
*But he just makes us sleepy."*

*Clap-snap. Clap-snap. Clap-snap-clap!*
Next Frankie stepped up onto the monkey bars and started to rap:

*"He shouldn't be a teacher.*
*He can't help us pass.*
*First we'll get him fired*
*Then we'll kick him in the—"*

"No swearing, Frankie," Mindy ordered. "Come on. You can come up with something else."
*Clap-snap. Clap-snap. Clap-snap-clap.*
Frankie kept thinking.
*Clap-snap. Clap-snap. Clap-snap-clap.*

He hit his head with his hands, trying to come up with a clean verse.

*Clap-snap. Clap-snap. Clap-snap-clap.*

"I give up." Frankie threw up his hands, climbed off the monkey bars, and sat down.

Mindy picked up the beat.

*Clap-snap. Clap-snap. Clap-snap-clap.*

> *"Mis-ter Finelli . . .*
> *I'm tellin you he'll blow it.*
> *Because we're so cool . . .*
> *And you know we show it."*

Cheers and the sound of palms slapping filled the playground.

"We have this essay thing aced!" Jeff danced around in circles.

"I bet they never had a rap essay before." Samantha laughed. "Mr. Finelli won't know what hit him."

"Let's keep it that way." Mindy spoke to the whole class. "Remember our ARF oath of silence."

"What oath of silence?" Frankie asked.

"Shhh." Mindy gave him a "shut up, you idiot" look.

"Oh, *that* oath of silence." Even Frankie knew by now that it was wise just to go along with Mindy when she was cooking up a scheme.

Mindy nodded and continued to cook. "We have

**65**

to keep up the dirty work so Mr. Finelli doesn't have time to start asking questions about the essay. I know"—Mindy snapped her fingers—"tonight we'll each do a different homework assignment. It'll drive him totally toxic. He won't have time to think about the essay contest, much less ask any questions about what we're doing to prepare for it."

It took a few minutes, but finally everybody knew what page of homework they were going to do that evening. Mindy couldn't wait to see Mr. Finelli's face when twenty-three different homework assignments were turned in at the same time. She had been very careful to make sure that no one was doing the page that had actually been assigned. That would have spoiled all the fun.

Soon the playground was almost empty. Only Frankie remained. He leaned back against the monkey bars, still trying to come up with another verse.

Twenty minutes later, he gave up and went home.

# Chapter Nine

**Over the next** week and a half Mindy, Frankie, and the rest of the class tried every trick they could think of to keep Mr. Finelli from thinking about the essay contest. The different-homework-assignment idea didn't quite work out as planned. Mr. Finelli just handed the assignments back the next day . . . fully corrected and graded. He congratulated the class on at least having done some homework, and he again complimented Mindy on her leadership skills. For two days after that she was depressed.

One day Frankie hid a plastic bag filled with chunky spaghetti sauce under his shirt. During a quiz he ripped it open with the end of his pencil and screamed in horror when the sauce started to ooze through the fabric.

"Oh, no!" Frankie grabbed his gooey middle. "My belly button's popped its cork!"

He tried to convince Mr. Finelli that he should definitely stop taking the quiz and go to the school nurse for a recorking. Instead Mr. Finelli handed him coupons for a box of spaghetti and garlic bread and told him that his shirt needed a little more oregano.

On another day Mr. Finelli had Max give a lecture on his favorite city: *Bone-os* Aires, Argentina, and his favorite rock group: Bone-jovi. For once Mindy couldn't think of a single way to ruin his lesson plan, so she just sat back and pretended to be bored out of her mind.

However, on the following Tuesday, Mindy and Samantha did have an idea about how to ruin the teacher's day. They sneaked into class early and glued everything on Mr. Finelli's desk firmly in place.

Later that day they both had to stay after school when they found they couldn't get up from their desks. Their jeans had somehow become glued to their seats. Their parents had to bring in new pairs for them to change into right at their desks before they could leave. The denim-covered seats were the talk of the school until Mindy threatened to mutilate the next person who even said the word *denim*.

It was pretty much dirty tricks as usual at Doverton School until three days before the essay contest. That was when the lunchroom exploded.

· · ·

There were three sixth-grade classes at Doverton School. Mr. Finelli's, Ms. Pendleton's, and Mrs. Moyer's. If Mr. Finelli's class was the worst, Mrs. Moyer's was the snobbiest. When the two groups got too close, it was like a grumpy grizzly bear and a tiger with a toothache trying to share a one-bedroom apartment. Odds were, there was going to be big trouble.

On a normal day the two classes rarely had any contact with each other, which was fine with both groups of students. The classrooms were down different hallways; each class had a different recess time; and at lunch Ms. Pendleton's class sat at the table between Mr. Finelli's and Mrs. Moyer's.

Then Ms. Pendleton's class took an all-day field trip to a radio station, and Ginny Piccolo was in a really nasty mood.

Everyone considered Ginny to be the snobbiest member of Mrs. Moyer's snob-filled class. She had perfect hair, perfect skin, perfect teeth, perfect clothes, and a perfectly horrible personality. Other than herself, Ginny really didn't like anyone. And she certainly did not like the students in Mr. Finelli's room.

With Ms. Pendleton's class away, there was nothing to separate Ginny from those she loved to hate most. There was one thing about Ginny Piccolo you could always count on: She never missed an opportunity to be a creep. This day was no exception.

"Can you believe they picked Finelli's class for the essay contest?" Ginny was sitting with her back toward Mindy, Frankie, and the rest. She pretended to be talking to her best friend, Donna ("My parents have a Jacuzzi . . . could you die?") Danielson and her boyfriend, Kile ("Duh") Duncan. But her voice was so loud that it could be heard half a lunchroom away.

"I mean, what were they thinking? Those Finelli-failures probably spell *essay* 'S.A.'" All the people in Mrs. Moyer's class started to laugh.

Meanwhile Frankie gripped his apple like it was a hardball. He was looking at Ginny as if she were the strike zone.

"Don't do it, Frankie," Mindy said. "She's not worth it. We don't want to get in trouble and get kicked out of the essay contest."

"What total geekazoids," Ginny said even louder. "Particularly that Jeff. I hear he flunked potty training three times and had to have a tutor." The laughter from Ginny's table filled the lunchroom.

Jeff started to get up, but Mindy stopped him. "She's a potty brain," Mindy whispered. "She's just mad we're in the essay contest and her class isn't."

"And that Samantha?" Ginny was almost squealing. "She's so dumb that she has a big sign on the ceiling of her room that says FEET FIRST, so she won't make a mistake getting out of bed in the morning."

One table laughed and one table didn't. Samantha, who had been taking karate classes for a year and a half, was going to offer to teach Ginny a lesson she'd never forget. But Mindy put her hand on her arm and said, "Forget it, Samantha. We have bigger things— Finelli things—to worry about."

Ginny leaned closer to her friends, but she kept talking in the same loud voice. "And this morning on the bus, Mindy pointed to some roadkill, but I said, 'That's not roadkill, that's your brother.' "

Without a word Mindy rose from the table and started walking toward Ginny. Mindy was beyond angry. Her mood had leapfrogged all the way to fury. No one tried to hold her back. Mindy's eyes were focused on the back of Ginny's head. No one reminded Mindy that she didn't have a brother.

Ginny and her friends were laughing so hard that they didn't notice Mindy approach. She walked up behind Ginny and started stroking her long hair. "What beautiful hair you have," Mindy said, sounding more like the Big Bad Wolf than an admirer of fine hair.

"Thank you." Ginny didn't pay any attention to who was giving her the compliment. Naturally people wanted to touch her hair. Ginny didn't give the person behind her a second thought. She should have.

"Really, really beautiful." As she stroked, Mindy

separated Ginny's hair to each side so that her neck was visible. Then, quicker than a pouncing cat, Mindy pulled the back of Ginny's white T-shirt toward her with one hand, and reached down and grabbed a completely full carton of chocolate milk with the other. In less than a blink and a half Mindy had poured the entire carton of chocolate milk down Ginny's back.

Before Ginny's scream could make it past her lips, Mindy slapped her on her now-squishy back. "How's that for roadkill, Ms. Ginny Pickanose?"

Ginny picked up a half-eaten slice of blueberry pie. Mindy ducked just in time. The pie flew over her head and landed smack in the center of Samantha's face.

Samantha, with blueberry goo dripping from her chin, whipped her tuna-salad-on-pita-bread sandwich through the air like a Frisbee. It barely missed Ginny, then made a direct hit in Kile's open mouth.

When the pita hit pay dirt, tuna splattered like pieces of a bomb. It covered Kile, the girl on his left, and the boy on his right. The three of them hurled their milk cartons toward Samantha.

Nobody had planned it. Nobody wanted it. Nobody thought it would ever really happen. But now nobody could stop it. The Great Doverton School Food War was under way, and there was no turning back.

Twinkies were launched, and frosting filled the air.

Someone dumped a cup of chocolate pudding down Jeff's jeans. Frankie mushed a peeled banana onto one boy's forehead and a peanut butter sandwich into another's hair. That was just before a jelly doughnut hit Frankie in the nose and exploded.

The other classes in the lunchroom dashed for cover and watched as a slice of chocolate cake caught one boy square in the ear. A girl, covered with SpaghettiOs from someone's thermos, screamed words one doesn't usually hear at lunch.

Even the noon aide, Mr. Kaylor, seemed too stunned to move, and he'd majored in mean in college. Ms. Mayflower, the gym teacher, knew that the last place you want to be in a food fight is sandwiched between the two sides. Unfortunately for her, she'd learned that lesson the hard way by walking between the tables to put an end to the battle. Not five seconds after she walked in, she walked out, covered with mayonnaise, Dorito dust, mustard, applesauce, Hawaiian Punch, strawberry low-fat yogurt, whipped cream, cold pizza, and a plum pit.

It looked like nothing short of a Ninja Turtle in a battle tank could stop the food-flinging frenzy.

Then a voice boomed through the lunchroom, "EVERYBODY FREEZE!"

The war came to an abrupt and immediate halt. Later some would swear that the food even stopped in midair. All eyes slowly turned toward the lunchroom door, eyes filled with fear because they knew what they were about to see.

At the door was a woman who stood four feet eleven inches on tiptoe. Her short bright red hair framed a face that featured a turned-up nose and rosy red cheeks. She might have reminded one of an elf, except for the fact that her eyes seemed to shoot fire wherever they gazed, and she was growling. It was Harriet Hackerman, better known as *Hatchet* Hackerman, the vice principal.

There were rumors that the VP had once been a teacher but that her class had mysteriously disappeared during a meat shortage. Others said a boy named Otto went into her office and came out a frog named Phillip. No one really believed she was a witch or anything. But then again, why did she seem to be absent every Halloween?

Mrs. Hackerman had received her nickname after a second-grader peeked into her car one day. He had immediately turned and run screaming into the school building. On the backseat he'd seen an ax, its blade covered with blood.

The vice principal had said the ax was just a prop for a play she was in the next week at the community center. Most of the students reacted by saying, "Oh, yeah. Sure. Right."

The Hatchet always carried a megaphone, which could really freak people out. Once a fifth-grader was having a nice private conversation with a friend in the hall, and the next thing she knew old Hatchet was standing three inches from her ear, screaming into the megaphone for her to get back to class. It was even more upsetting—and embarrassing—when she poked open the boys' bathroom door with her megaphone and let those inside know that they'd better hurry.

One of the Hatchet's favorite targets was anyone from Mr. Finelli's class. This year she had been strongly opposed to letting the top four troublemakers —Mindy, Jeff, Samantha, and Frankie—into Doverton School, but she'd been outvoted. Since school had begun, she'd been trying to get at them and their teacher whatever way she could. She didn't like the students in Room 201, and she also didn't like the teacher. But up till now she hadn't been able to do anything about it.

On the day of the food fight Ginny ran up, sobbing, to the Hatchet. "Oh, Mrs. Hackerman. Look what they did to us." Ginny pointed at Mr. Finelli's class. "And we didn't do anything to deserve it."

"Liar!" Frankie, Mindy, and about half of their classmates yelled together.

"Shut up!" Hatchet Hackerman yelled alone. She was known to play favorites, and one of her special pets was Ginny Piccolo.

The Hatchet put her arm around Ginny, but yanked it back when she felt the chocolate milk still

**75**

dripping from the back of Ginny's shirt. "Poor little thing," the VP cooed, sounding like a demon trying to imitate a dove. "You just tell your good buddy which hooligan in Finelli's class fired the first Fig Newton."

With fake tears streaming down her face, Ginny pointed to Frankie, Jeff, Mindy, and Samantha. "Those four. They started it because they hate me."

"At least she got it half right," Samantha whispered.

Ginny looked up at her beloved Hatchet-hero. "Aren't you going to do something about it? Please, please, pretty please, do something. I'm so scared."

"You bet I'm going to do something." Mrs. Hackerman glared at the four whom Ginny had fingered. "My office . . . NOW. You troublemakers will wish you were frogs before I'm through with you."

"See, I told you it was true about the frog named Phillip," Frankie tried to say without moving his lips.

"Shut up, toad face," Jeff said. "We're in enough trouble already."

Mrs. Hackerman gestured toward the rest of Mr. Finelli's class. "Clean up this place. I want to be able to see the reflection of my face in the floor."

"Why?" Mindy whispered.

"What was that, Missy?"

Mindy had to think fast. "I said 'Bye.' We were just leaving for your office. Bye, bye." Mindy and her three friends walked out of the lunchroom as quickly as possible.

The Hatchet turned toward Ginny's class. "Now, you students get cleaned up and go back to class. Your attackers will be punished."

"Thank you, Mrs. Hackerman," the entire class chanted as they rose from their seats.

When Mrs. Hackerman wasn't looking, Ginny knocked over one last carton of milk. As the white liquid poured onto the floor, Ginny looked at the people from Mr. Finelli's class. "Make sure you clean everything up. And put a smile on your faces. . . . There's no use in crying over spilled milk."

Ginny took one step forward but didn't look where she was stepping. Her foot hit the milk and flew up into the air, pulling the rest of her body along for the ride. When she finally landed, Ginny lay flat on her back in a bed of 2 percent milk and smushed lasagna, which had been the hot lunch of the day.

Everyone in Mr. Finelli's class cheered.

The Hatchet whirled around, shooting sparks at them with her eyes. "Detention, all of you, until you're able to drive," she snapped, and then stormed out of the lunchroom.

# Chapter Ten

Frankie rubbed some jelly off his chin. Mindy brushed potato-chip crumbs from her hair. Samantha pulled a blueberry out of her nose, and Jeff paced back and forth, trying to shake the chocolate pudding down his pant leg. As they waited in Hatchet Hackerman's office, they all realized that they'd never been more nervous or scared in their entire lives.

Samantha, Jeff, and Mindy were worried about what their parents were going to say. All Frankie kept thinking was "ribbit, ribbit, ribbit." He also wondered if it was possible to order a double-fly-and-cheese pizza from Pizza Hut. Being turned into a frog might be okay, but giving up pizza would be real torture.

• • •

Down the hall from the office and around two corners, Mrs. Hackerman was whistling while she walked. She cracked her knuckles and thanked her lucky lollipops that she was a vice principal. "I love days like this!" she said out loud as she turned the first corner.

Mrs. Hackerman was far too pleased with herself to watch where she was going. Besides, she could safely assume that people would always get out of her way. But as with many assumptions, this one eventually was proven wrong. As soon as the vice principal turned the next corner, she ran headfirst into Mr. Finelli.

The crash could be heard as far away as the library. Mr. Finelli banged against a row of lockers. Mrs. Hackerman took a seat on the hallway floor—in the exact spot where David Matthews had thrown up a half hour earlier.

Mr. Finelli offered her a hand to help her up. "Well, Mrs. Hatch . . . er, I mean Hackerman." Mr. Finelli smiled. "How nice to run into you."

The Hatchet batted his hand away and stood up. "You call yourself a teacher?" She stood nose-to-nose with him and shrieked. "You're pitiful. Your class is pitiful. I have them now, Mr. Finelli. What do you think about that? And when I'm through with your class of clods, I'm coming for you."

"And my little dog too?" Mr. Finelli asked.

"Your what?" Obviously Mrs. Hackerman had never seen *The Wizard of Oz*.

Before Mr. Finelli could explain, the Hatchet stormed past him. As she did, Mr. Finelli coughed twice. That was the signal. Two third-graders immediately came around another corner and forced Mrs. Hackerman to stop in her tracks.

"Mrs. Hackerman! Mrs. Hackerman! Come quick!" one said.

"Move it or lose it, kid. I have work to do." The Hatchet tried to duck around to the right, but the students moved right along with her and kept blocking the way.

"But Mrs. Hackerman, Mrs. Hackerman! We need you!" the other third-grader pleaded.

"Look, a UFO!" Mrs. Hackerman pointed toward the ceiling and tried to dash around to the left. The students matched her dash for dash. After pointing to imaginary circus clowns, ice-cream trucks, and rock groups and still failing to get around the two students, Hatchet Hackerman gave up. "Oh, all right. What is it already?"

"It's Bobby Curtis. He's trying to flush his arm down the toilet again."

"Yeah," the other student joined in. "He's locked himself in the teachers' bathroom. He says the only way he's coming out is through the pipes."

If Mrs. Hackerman had been paying attention, she

would have heard the giggling that came from around the corner. That was where Bobby Curtis was hiding. He just loved playing tricks on the Hatchet.

Simply put, Bobby was trouble with a capital *T*. He was most famous for the time he'd stood up on his desk and mooned his first-grade class when the teacher was out of the room. Unfortunately for him his teacher walked in just in time to get to the bottom of the story.

Bobby was certainly a strong candidate for future admission to Mr. Finelli's class. So, trying to flush himself down the toilet was a real possibility. Mrs. Hackerman had no choice but to take the threat to the school's plumbing system seriously.

She fully intended to tell Mr. Finelli that he and his class were still firmly on her hook and that this Bobby problem would only delay their ultimate punishment. But when she turned around, Mr. Finelli was gone.

When the door to Mrs. Hackerman's office flew open, the four students waiting inside almost jumped out of their underwear. Everyone gasped, except for Frankie, who let out a scared, high-pitched "Ribbit."

"Well, Ribbit back at-cha." Mr. Finelli laughed as he walked through the door. He looked at the food-covered four and said, "Yeech, you are all a mess."

"Thanks for noticing," Mindy said with all the sarcasm her mustard-coated mouth could muster. "Did you come to see the execution?"

"No, to prevent it if you'll let me." Mr. Finelli reached outside the office door and pulled in two knapsacks. One was green and one was tan. He handed the green one to Jeff and Frankie and the tan one to Samantha and Mindy. He also pulled four washcloths out of his pocket and handed one to each student. "Go into the bathrooms. Change your clothes and clean up. Better hurry, before the Hatchet returns."

Samantha and Mindy ran out of the office and darted down the hall to the girls' bathroom, which was only two doors away. Jeff and Frankie ran in the other direction to the boys' bathroom. When the students opened their respective knapsacks, they found that they contained clothing that just happened to be the right size.

At the other end of the building Hatchet Hackerman kicked in the door to the teachers' bathroom. After a few minutes she'd given up on trying to talk Bobby out. No matter what she said, or what threats she made, Bobby wouldn't say a word or open the locked door.

Little did she know that Bobby was actually halfway across the school happily throwing spitballs in his classroom. The Hatchet remained convinced he was trying to take a trip on the Sewer Line Express.

"I have you now," Mrs. Hackerman said as she charged into the bathroom like a pit bull with personality problems. The two students who'd led her there followed closely behind and tried not to laugh. It wasn't easy.

Mrs. Hackerman stormed around the bathroom in search of Bobby. She was growling, she was shaking, she was almost foaming at the mouth. She slammed open stall after stall. Finally she got to the very last one. Mrs. Hackerman paused. A huge, ugly smile came to her lips. "You flushed your last flush, Mr. Funny Man. Ready or not . . . here I come."

The Hatchet slammed the door to the last stall open. She froze in her tracks. Bobby wasn't there. All she saw was his Baltimore Orioles baseball cap spinning around in the swirling water.

Meanwhile the two students had come up close behind the vice principal. One of them peeked over Mrs. Hackerman's shoulder. He looked back at his friend with a fake shocked expression on his face and said, "Brad, you're not going to believe it."

"Believe what?"

"I think Bobby made it."

Mrs. Hackerman yowled and raced out of the lounge and toward her office.

• • •

Mindy, Frankie, Jeff, and Samantha dashed back to Mrs. Hackerman's office in their clean clothes just moments before the Hatchet clomped in through the door. She was madder than usual and meaner than ever.

Mr. Finelli decided to step in. "Where have you been, Mrs. Hackerman? We've been waiting and waiting."

"Well, you're going to have to wait a little longer." The Hatchet didn't even look at Mr. Finelli, or the four sixth-graders. She just mumbled her way over to her telephone.

"Is anything wrong?" Mr. Finelli asked.

"If you must know, Bobby Curtis flushed himself down the toilet. Now, don't bother me, I have to call a plumber."

Mrs. Hackerman started dialing the telephone. She reached the last number when Bobby walked in. "My teacher said to give you these field-trip permission slips." Bobby handed Mrs. Hackerman an envelope and left the office, his perfectly dry Baltimore Orioles baseball cap resting comfortably on his head.

Mrs. Hackerman's jaw dropped open so far, Mindy could see her tonsils dancing back and forth. Then the vice principal snapped it shut like a bear trap. "Very funny, Bobby!" she shouted after him. "You didn't fool me for a second." Mrs. Hackerman slowly hung up the phone and stared at the door.

"Excuse me, Mrs. Hackerman," Mr. Finelli began, "but why are we here? Is there a problem?"

Eagerly the Hatchet turned toward the next people on her hit list. Mindy knew she'd been dying to make the students squirm and beg for mercy. Instead, when she saw them, her jaw dropped open again and hit her chest.

"Does that happen often?" Mr. Finelli sounded very concerned. "I know a good jaw doctor if you want someone to take a look at it."

Mrs. Hackerman couldn't believe her eyes. Jeff, Samantha, Frankie, and Mindy were now neatly dressed in totally clean clothing. There wasn't a speck of egg salad or strawberry yogurt on them. There wasn't a crumb of evidence to convict them of their crimes. "Nice trick, but it won't work," Mrs. Hackerman scolded them with a sneer. "You're not going to get away with it. I saw what you did."

"What did they do?" Mr. Finelli asked.

"You know very well what they did. I know someone told you about the food fight."

"Food fight?" Jeff looked confused.

"Like, with real food?" Samantha asked.

"Ugh, gross." Mindy wrinkled her nose.

"Any leftovers?" Frankie sounded hopeful.

Mr. Finelli gestured at the members of his class. "They sure don't look like they were in a food fight. I mean, just look at their clothes. They're perfectly clean."

At that point the school principal, Ms. Darlene McAlister, walked into the office. "What's going on?" she asked. "Why aren't these students in class?"

Mr. Finelli was about to answer when Hatchet Hackerman stepped in front of him. "I'll tell you what's going on. These four hoodlums started a food fight in the cafeteria."

Ms. McAlister looked at the four. "They sure don't look like they were in a food fight. I mean, just look at their clothes. They're perfectly clean."

Mrs. Hackerman looked at Mr. Finelli, who just shrugged. She grabbed the principal's hand. "I'll prove it to you." Mrs. Hackerman's eyes narrowed and her nostrils flared. "Follow me."

The Hatchet led the way to the lunchroom, followed by Ms. McAlister, Mr. Finelli, Mindy, Samantha, Jeff, and finally Frankie.

When the vice principal reached the lunchroom door, she stopped. "Now you'll see that the proof really is in the pudding . . . and the pudding is all over the walls, floor, and ceiling."

Mrs. Hackerman triumphantly flung open the door. "Ah huh!" she snarled loudly. "Oh no," she whimpered softly. The lunchroom was sparkling clean from top to bottom. The tables gleamed and the floor glistened like the surface of an ice-skating rink. There wasn't so much as a drop of Twinkie goo anywhere.

"W-wait," Mrs. Hackerman stammered. "I have witnesses." She spent the next few minutes searching for the noon aide, who'd already left, and Ms. Mayflower, the gym teacher. What the Hatchet didn't know was that Ms. Mayflower was so embarrassed over what had happened during the food fight that she'd crawled behind a rack of baseball bats and under a pile of tumbling mats and planned to stay there till school let out.

"Never mind the lunchroom," Hatchet finally hooted. She grabbed Principal McAlister's hand once again. "Follow me." This time Mrs. Hackerman led the group to Mr. Finelli's classroom. "I don't know how these four did it," she mumbled, "but wait until you see the rest of the junior criminals in this class." She slammed the door open. "Ah ha!" she shrieked. "Oh no!" she cried.

All of the students were seated at their desks quietly reading. Their clothing looked brand-new and sparkling clean. Max was sitting behind Mr. Finelli's desk. He held a diet book in his hands.

"Shhh," Mr. Finelli whispered. "This is P.R.T.— private reading time." No one noticed the large pile of knapsacks in the corner.

"Never mind the classroom," Hatchet howled,

and grabbed the principal's hand. "Follow me to Mrs. Moyer's room. Then you'll know the truth."

This time Ms. McAlister shook free. "The truth is," the principal said, "I think I know enough already."

"But-but-but-but-but-but-but—" Mrs. Hackerman sounded like a motor boat with engine trouble.

"No but-but-buts about it," Principal McAlister said as she started leading Mrs. Hackerman away. "You look tired, very tired. Maybe you could use a little rest. How about a nice long vacation?"

When Mrs. Hackerman looked up at the principal, she raised her eyebrows and sounded hopeful. "I've always wanted to visit Antarctica."

"Splendid," everyone heard Ms. McAlister reply. "I understand the one-way fares are quite reasonable this time of year."

The two exited the classroom and disappeared from sight.

Mr. Finelli stood at the front of the classroom and took a bow.

Everyone except Max cheered. The skeleton's head was now resting on the open book on the desk, while his body still sat upright in the chair. "That Max." Mr. Finelli walked over and put the skeleton's head back in place. "He always loses his head over a good book."

"Psst, hey, Mindy," Frankie whispered. "The dude saved our butts, maybe we should—"

"Quiet," Mindy whispered hastily. "I know what Fin-belly's trying to do. Trust me."

Mindy really had no idea what Mr. Finelli was trying to do. Sure, he saved them from the Hatchet, but why? It had to be some kind of trick, she thought. She just needed to figure out what it was.

Just then there was a knock at the classroom door, and it opened wide enough for a head to pop through. The head that did the popping belonged to the principal. "I'm so sorry to interrupt." She smiled. "But could I possibly see you for just a minute or two, Mr. Finelli? I'd like to discuss Mrs. Hackerman's . . . uh . . . uh . . . travel plans."

"Of course"—Mr. Finelli turned to the class—"P.R.T's been held over by popular demand. Try not to miss me."

Mindy knew she would never *miss* a teacher. But she also knew that Mr. Finelli was one teacher she'd never forget.

# Chapter Eleven

**By the next morning** Mindy had decided she had to do something to get the anti-Finelli spirit going strong again, or they could kiss the essay-contest plan good-bye. It was her best teacher-torturing idea yet, and she wasn't about to abandon it.

Mindy got her chance to rally her classmates when Mr. Finelli went next door to borrow some chalk.

"That man is really starting to bug me," she announced as soon as Mr. Finelli closed the door behind him. "We've got to get to work. We have only three days. If we want to rock-and-roll Mr. Fink-elli right on out of here, we've got to polish our rap."

Mindy raised her fist into the air. She expected everyone to cheer and clap their approval. Instead no one said a word. Not one yippee, yea, or even little yahoo could be heard. Mindy stood up and went to the head of the classroom. "What is wrong with you? That Mr. Pot-belli does one thing right and you all turn to wimps?"

"Hey," Frankie said. "Nobody calls me a—"

Frankie didn't get to finish his protest. Mindy had the floor and wasn't even close to giving it up. "I don't get it and I don't like it. You've all been wussified."

A boy toward the back stood up. "I don't know what the rest of you guys think, but I feel what Mr. Finelli did yesterday was really cool."

Most of the class nodded in agreement.

Everyone expected Mindy to explode with anger. Instead an extremely calm expression spread over her face. She slowly started walking toward the boy, whose discomfort increased with every step she took. He nervously shifted his weight from one foot to the other. His eyes darted from side to side, searching for someplace to duck to when Mindy attacked. She moved in closer. He started to sweat.

Mindy walked up next to him. His body tensed. He closed his eyes. He felt Mindy's hand on his shoulder. He heard her say, "You know, you're right. It was cool."

The boy almost fainted. "I'm what?"

"He's what?" Four other class members echoed. The entire class was shocked.

"Mindy, are you saying that Mr. Finelli is . . . cool?" Frankie asked in total disbelief.

"No. Of course not," Mindy said.

"Phew." Frankie wiped his brow. "I thought we were going to have to call E.M.S."

"What he *did* was cool."

"What's the number for E.M.S.?" Frankie punched Jeff on the arm.

"Look it up." Jeff rubbed his arm.

"Okay. How do you spell it?"

Jeff's attention had returned to what Mindy was saying. He didn't answer Frankie's last question.

"Sure, it was cool to cover for us." Mindy walked back to the front of the classroom. "But I think he's still as shifty, sneaky, and snaky as ever."

"Then why did he do it?" a boy in the back asked.

"It was all a trick," Mindy answered. "A trick to get us to like him."

"Why?"

"Does the boy need a brain transplant, or what?" Mindy huffed. "Any donors?"

Frankie started to raise his hand, but changed his mind.

"It's really simple," Mindy said. "He wants us to like him so we'll write nice things about him in the essay. Think about it. He'll do anything to get us to say on TV what a great teacher he is. If we do, maybe he thinks he can get a raise or something. Everything he does is a trick, like naming that stupid skeleton Max and pretending that he can talk."

A sudden gust of wind swept in the window, causing Max to sway. His jaws began to click and his bones rattled. A couple of students jumped. Mindy slammed the window shut. Max's head fell off his body and rolled into a corner. This time lots of students jumped.

"What a bunch of fraidy-geeks." Mindy giggled. "It's just another trick. Finelli is a magician. He could probably make Frankie's head roll into a corner."

Frankie grabbed his head and dug his fingers into his scalp.

Mindy looked over the class. "Get with it, people. Maybe we should change the class cheer to 'We're wimps . . . you know it . . . We're dweebs . . . we show it.' "

Frankie, Jeff, and several others joined in a chorus of "No way!" Then Mindy moved in for the kill.

"Remember the toupee in the fish tank? Remember how he made us all just sit here all day?" She walked up to a girl in the third row. "Lisa, just how badly *did* you have to go to the bathroom that day?" Mindy went up to a boy near the windows. "Harold, remember how you had to miss baseball practice, and how someone else took your place in the lineup?" Mindy raced over to Frankie. "And remember how he made you miss your lunch?"

"She's right." Frankie leapt to his feet. "The man has got to go!"

Everyone started to talk at the same time, each giving his or her opinion of their teacher.

At that exact moment Mr. Finelli opened the door and stuck his head into the room. He and the teacher next door were still looking for chalk. "Settle down in there." Mr. Finelli sounded annoyed.

Everybody kept mumbling.

"Need some settling-down motivation?" Mr. Finelli asked. "I've got it." He snapped his fingers. "Math test in fifteen minutes. How's that for motivation?"

"Pretty good, I think." Mr. Finelli was carrying on a conversation with himself.

"Thank you," Mr. Finelli said.

"You're welcome," Mr. Finelli responded.

"You know," Mr. Finelli continued his one-person dialogue. "If I were having a math test in fifteen minutes, I'd be studying instead of goofing around, wouldn't I?"

"Indeed I would," he responded just before pulling his head out of the classroom and closing the door.

Mindy couldn't believe her luck. She had needed something to completely convince her classmates that Finelli had to go, and what more convincing argument could there be than a test?

She clapped her hands twice to get everyone's at-

**94**

tention. "Let's vote. All in favor of rapping Mr. Test-elli say 'aye.'"

*Ayes* filled the room.

"Opposed?"

The room remained totally silent.

"Motion carried." Mindy smiled smugly. "Unanimously."

For the next two days Jeff, Samantha, Frankie, and Mindy worked on the rap night and day. Each of them went over his or her own verses to make them as nasty and funny as possible. The plan was for the rest of the class to join in on the chorus.

Finally, their essay about what they liked about their teacher was ready to be rapped.

Mindy started the rehearsal:

*Clap-snap. Clap-snap. Clap-snap-clap.*

> *"Our teacher's so mean,*
> *He bathes in witches' brew.*
> *We think he's a monster,*
> *Soon you will too.*

> *"This essay's our chance*
> *To bring the story out.*
> *So hold on to your pants*
> *And hear what he's about."*

*Clap-snap. Clap-snap. Clap-snap-clap!*
Samantha, Jeff, and Frankie joined in on the chorus:

> *"Mis-ter Finelli.*
> *They say he can teach.*
> *But he smells like a skunk,*
> *And he looks like a crea . . . ture."*

*Clap-snap. Clap-snap. Clap-snap-clap!*
Jeff picked up his verse:

> *"Mis-ter Finelli.*
> *His hair is a wig.*
> *His nose is like Pinocchio's,*
> *He eats just like a pig."*

*Clap-snap. Clap-snap. Clap-snap-clap!*
Samantha stepped forward:

> *"He ain't no teacher,*
> *He ain't so cool.*
> *We hate his every feature,*
> *Get him out of our school."*

*Clap-snap. Clap-snap. Clap-snap-clap!*

*"Mis-ter Finelli.*
*They say he can teach.*
*But he smells like a skunk,*
*And he looks like a crea . . . ture."*

*Clap-snap. Clap-snap. Clap-snap-clap!*
Mindy took the next verse:

*"He thinks he's Napoleon,*
*He talks to bones named Max.*
*Our problems keep on rollin' in,*
*With each dumb joke he cracks."*

*Clap-snap. Clap-snap. Clap-snap-clap!*
Frankie stepped forward with his new verse:

*"He shouldn't be a teacher.*
*He can't help us pass.*
*He really makes us tired,*
*Because he gives us gas."*

*Clap-snap. Clap-snap. Clap-snap-clap!*

*"Mis-ter Finelli.*
*They say he can teach.*
*But he smells like a skunk,*
*And he looks like a crea . . . ture."*

*Clap-snap. Clap-snap. Clap-snap-clap!*

Mindy had one more verse that she insisted on doing alone:

> *"He doesn't teach—he tortures.*
> *He's one big grumpy crank.*
> *Yawn once and he will make you*
> *Stick your arm in the fish tank."*

*Clap-snap. Clap-snap. Clap-snap-clap!*

In the last verse each person took one line. Jeff rapped first, followed by Frankie, Samantha, and finally Mindy:

> *"He deserves to be fired."*
> *"Throw the bum out."*
> *"Before he takes us good, sweet kids"*
> *"And turns us into trout."*

*Clap-snap. Clap-snap. Clap-snap-clap!*

After the last *Clap-snap-clap!* everyone made fish faces and pretended to swim around the room. It was the perfect way to end the rap.

The four rappers fell to the floor laughing.

"Look out, Mr. Finelli . . . we're comin' at-cha and going strong!" Mindy shouted.

"We'll make essay history!" Samantha cheered.

"We'll run that teacher out of town by sundown!" Jeff said, imitating a sheriff in the Wild West while he rolled around on his back and kicked his feet.

All Frankie could think to say was "Woof!" But he said it over and over again, and he said it very well.

# Chapter Twelve

**When the Action** to Reject Finelli Committee performed the rap for the rest of their class, they received a standing ovation. Mr. Finelli was finally going to get what he royally deserved. Now the class couldn't wait for the contest to begin. Every hour seemed to last two, but finally the day of the essay contest arrived.

The competition was going to be held at Harrison High School because it had the biggest auditorium in the school district. Every sixth-grade class in the district was being bussed in. The judges included two high school principals, an assistant to the mayor, a newspaper editor, and a news anchorwoman and a weatherman from the station that was broadcasting the event.

When Frankie, Mindy, Jeff, Samantha, and the rest of Mr. Finelli's class walked into the auditorium, there were lights, electrical cables, technicians, teachers, and confusion everywhere. The TV people pulled Mr. Finelli aside and directed the class toward the stage.

"Like the chimp said to the ape in the monkey house," Frankie joked, "this place is a zoo."

"Shut up, Gorilla-breath," Samantha teased.

"Me Tarzan!" Frankie banged on his chest.

"No, no." Mindy shook her head. "Me Mindy . . . you stupid."

"I might be dumb." Frankie laughed. "But I ain't stupid." On another day Frankie might have been hurt by what Mindy had said. But today he was in the best mood he'd been in since last week, when he and Jeff had ordered a large pizza and Jeff had had to go home before it arrived.

Besides, teacher bashing always made Frankie smile. Even though he secretly thought Mr. Finelli was okay, he certainly wasn't about to say anything and ruin the fun—or worse, make Mindy mad at him.

Except for when Frankie burped into the microphone, the rehearsal went very smoothly. They didn't have to read their essays yet, just practice walking up onstage so they'd know where to go when the lights were on and the cameras were rolling. The students chosen to do the actual reading were supposed to stand in front of their whole class. Mindy was ecstatic —the format was good for reading an essay, but it was fabulous for reciting a rap.

Finally it was time. Several juniors from the high school led the classes who were about to compete to the gym to wait their turn. All the sixth-grade teachers in the district were going to be introduced before the first essay was presented. They were taken in the other direction.

In the gym the name of each school was printed on a poster board and hung on the wall. The students were supposed to gather in the taped-off square area beneath their school's name. Everyone followed the rules. . . . Well, almost everyone.

Mr. Finelli's class was scheduled to be the next-to-last group to perform. After about a minute and a half of waiting, Mindy became hopelessly bored. She needed to escape. "Frankie," she whispered. When he didn't respond, she whispered louder. "Frankie!" When he still didn't answer, she poked him in the back.

Frankie released the kid he had in a headlock and whined, "What? You don't have to get violent, you know."

Mindy whispered into his ear, "Let's blow this Popsicle stand and see what this high school is really like. Pass it on."

Frankie turned and whispered into Samantha's ear.

She gave him a strange look before passing the message along. Finally, when it was whispered to Jeff, he looked totally confused. Jeff walked up to Mindy. "You want to go stand on a blue Pop-Tart in the high school cafeteria, like now?"

Mindy didn't answer. She just grabbed Frankie and Jeff by the arms and pushed them toward the side door of the gym. "Come on," she whispered to Samantha, "let's have some fun."

Samantha checked to make sure that the high school juniors who'd been assigned the job of keeping an eye on the gym weren't looking before she followed her friends out the door.

The four ARF Committee members found themselves in a long, dark hallway that came to a dead end to the left. Along the hallway were three doors. One led back into the gym. The other doors were to the men's and women's locker rooms. The men's was to the left, the women's to the right.

"This way." Mindy pointed to the right.

The four explorers walked past the men's locker-room door and were almost to the end of the hall when they heard voices and footsteps coming from around the corner. Everyone froze in his or her tracks. The voices and the footsteps were getting closer—quickly.

"See who it is," Mindy whispered to Frankie.

"Why should *I* go see?" he whispered back.

"Because you're the brave one."

"Oh, yeah, I forgot." While trying to stop his knees from shaking, Frankie crawled on his belly and peeked around the corner. He shot up like a rocket and raced back to Mindy, Samantha, and Jeff. "It's the heat," he frantically whispered.

"Speak English for once." Samantha rolled her eyes.

"It's the sixth-grade t-teachers," Frankie stammered.

"Which ones?" Jeff asked.

"All of them . . . and they're coming this way."

Everyone did the next logical thing. They turned and ran. Unfortunately they all turned in opposite directions and ended up running into each other.

"Back to the gym," Jeff called.

"We'll never make it. It's too far," Frankie cried.

Mindy looked around. They had only one choice. She pointed toward the men's locker room. "Hurry."

"I'm not going in there." Samantha was shocked. "That's for guys."

The footsteps and voices were getting closer and closer. Everyone looked at Samantha, who folded her arms. "I'm still not going in th—"

With one mighty shove from Mindy, Samantha found herself almost flying through the door to the men's locker room. Frankie, Jeff, and Mindy followed her and closed the door just as the teachers rounded the corner and started down the hall.

Mindy and Frankie leaned up against some lockers and tried to catch their breath. Jeff and Samantha sat down on a bench and did the same thing. "That was close," Samantha panted.

"Too close," Jeff corrected.

They didn't know it for another few seconds, but their close encounter had just begun.

Suddenly the door to the locker room was flung open, and every sixth-grade teacher in the district walked in.

There were eight rows of lockers in the Harrison High locker room. At the sound of the teachers approaching the locker-room door, Mindy and Company had dashed down one of them. Luckily for them the teachers settled down on the benches right near the door.

While the teachers talked and complained about having to wait in the locker room until they were introduced to the audience in the auditorium, the four students tried not to breathe. Suddenly one particularly loud and annoying male teacher's voice filled the air. Frankie recognized it right away. "Mr. Nowak," Frankie said under his breath. "That gunk-head."

Mr. Nowak was a sixth-grade teacher at Frankie's old school. Frankie remembered back to when he was a first-grader. He had been late for school and was running down the hall to get to class. Frankie could still hear Mr. Nowak's voice screaming, "Slow down, junior-jerk. We have rules about running, or can't you read?"

Mr. Nowak was best known for his habit of rubbing his eyebrows and watching the dandruff fall onto his desk. His class had been picked to write an essay for the contest, and being the rotten sport that he was, Mr. Nowak always looked out for a chance to insult the competition.

"Hey, Finelli," his voice boomed, "how much did you have to pay to have them pick your class of loony-bird losers?"

"Loony-bird losers?" Frankie growled softly. "That from a guy who makes dandruff piles for a hobby?"

"Shhh," Mindy said. For once she was actually interested in hearing what a teacher had to say.

Mr. Finelli laughed. "What exactly is a 'loony-bird,' Mr. Nowak?"

"I don't know," Mr. Nowak answered. "But you have a whole flock of them in your class."

When Mr. Nowak finished laughing at his own joke, he went right on talking. "Why don't you just give up and go home now, before you embarrass yourself?"

"Don't count your chickens before the essays are

hatched," Mr. Finelli's said calmly. "My class is full of surprises."

Mindy couldn't believe her ears. A teacher defending them against another teacher? *Nah*, she thought. *It has to be a trick.*

"Well, you can count on this," Mr. Nowak said smugly. "Your class of preteenage mutant nincompoop nobodies doesn't stand a chance. Talk about America's *least* wanted. I mean, nobody wanted them but you, Finelli. I guess it takes one to teach one."

Mindy looked at Frankie. His beet-red face and grinding teeth made it clear that he was trying to control his temper.

"I guess we'll just let the essays do the talking, okay?" Mr. Finelli spoke in very even tones.

"Oh, those essays will talk, all right. I just hope there's a translator present for your class. I don't think very many of us speak Duh-wanese." Mr. Nowak was the only one in the locker room laughing, but he was laughing so hard that he didn't even notice.

"You won't laugh when my class beats yours," Mr. Finelli said matter-of-factly.

"His class what?" Jeff said, almost loudly enough for the teachers to hear.

"Your class what?" Mr. Nowak said.

"When my class finishes ahead of yours," Mr. Finelli stated boldly.

"He's totally whacked," Samantha whispered.

"I've got all honor students in my class, Finelli. Yours are all dishonor."

Mindy strained to hear as Mr. Nowak lowered his voice and said, "Anybody got a thermometer? This boy has got to have one granddaddy of a fever."

"Never felt better," Mr. Finelli piped up.

"You got yourself a big mouth, Finelli," Mr. Nowak said. "But are you ready to back up your words with a little wager? What are you willing to give up if your class of clowns loses to mine? Which, I think any sane person would agree, it will."

Mr. Finelli was quiet for a second. "How about my job?"

Samantha turned to the others, her eyes as wide as saucers. "His job?" she said.

"Shhh!" Mindy shushed her. "I want to hear what's going to happen."

"You are on." Mr. Nowak clapped his hands and did a little dance.

"Wait just a second," Mr. Finelli said. "What will *you* give up if my class does beat yours?"

"I'll tell you what, Finelli. If your class beats my class, you can have anything you want. And if not"— Mr. Nowak snorted—"I get your teaching certificate on a silver platter."

Mr. Finelli smiled, and shook Mr. Nowak's hand. "It's a bet."

# Chapter Thirteen

**Thirty seconds later** there was a knock on the locker-room door and the teachers were called to the auditorium. As they filed out, the four students heard Mr. Nowak say, "Don't worry, old man. You can always have a job cutting my grass. And my bathroom needs a good cleaning."

All Mr. Finelli said was, "I bet it does."

As soon as the teachers had all left the locker room, Mindy turned to the others. "Let's get out of here." She led the way back to the gym.

Behind her Samantha, Jeff, and Frankie were carrying on their own private conversation.

"Did you hear what Mr. Finelli said?" Jeff whispered.

"Yeah, I ain't never had a teacher stick up for me

before." Frankie shook his head. "The dude didn't back down from the Hatchet or Mr. Nowak."

"He put his job on the line for us." Samantha was genuinely impressed.

"Yeah. And if we lose to Nowak's class, we might get someone just like Nowak for our teacher." Frankie shivered.

"Or someone like Hatchet Hackerman," Jeff added.

"I think we should change the rap," Samantha said cautiously. The three of them glanced up at Mindy. "Go ahead, Frankie," Samantha urged. "Tell her we're going to change the rap."

Frankie decided right then and there to give up the title of "The Brave One." "Jeff, I name you 'The Brave One.' You tell her."

"Samantha, you do it," Jeff said nervously. "You're a girl."

"And you're a boy," Samantha said.

"You're all a bunch of chickens." Suddenly Mindy stopped and turned to face them.

As she listened to her friends talking, Mindy actually did have second thoughts about the rap. *Remember what it felt like to be kissed on the elbow by a goldfish with your arm sunk deep in a slimy fish tank*, she reminded herself. Totally embarrassing. She just couldn't let Mr. Finelli get away with it. "We are not changing the rap. No way, no how, na-uh, forget it!"

"But Mindy. Look what he did for us," Jeff said.

"Yeah," Frankie agreed. "He bet his job on us."

"You know," Samantha added softly, "Mr. Nowak was right about one thing."

"What?" all three of her friends said together.

"No one else wanted us . . . except Mr. Finelli."

"Oh, boo-hoo, and quickly now, double time, boo-hoo-hoo." Mindy sobbed sarcastically. "I think all of you are forgetting one thing."

"And that is?" Samantha asked.

"You're forgetting what he is."

"Who?" Jeff asked.

"Mr. Finelli."

"What Mr. Finelli is?" Frankie asked.

"Yeah." Mindy crossed her arms and asked her question. "What is he?"

"A teacher," Samantha, Jeff, and Frankie answered.

"Nuff said." Mindy ended the discussion.

When they got back to the gym, Frankie told the rest of the class what had happened. Mindy's only comments were "So what?" and "Big deal." No matter what anyone said, no one could change Mindy's mind. She didn't want to hear the change-the-rap arguments. She wasn't about to admit that she'd been wrong about a teacher.

Finally, after about an hour-long wait, it was Mr.

Finelli's class's turn to go onstage. As they filed toward the auditorium, Frankie walked next to Mindy. "Just think about it, okay? Just think about it."

"I've already done more than enough thinking about Mr. Jerk-elli. Now it's party time."

"But . . ." Another boy tried to argue the point.

"But—out!" Mindy snapped. "It's too late to change anything anyway."

Five minutes later Mindy, Frankie, Jeff, and Samantha were standing onstage, with their entire class behind them. The TV lights were bright and hot. The master of ceremonies was an English teacher who had dreams of being a late-night talk-show host. He introduced Mr. Finelli's class.

"Now, representing Doverton School, with our second-from-last essay, let's give it up for the class from Room Two-oh-one." The man circled his fist in front of himself and said, "Whoo-whoo-whoo." The audience applauded politely.

Mindy stepped up to the microphone. She looked at the audience. She spotted Mr. Nowak, who nudged the person next to him with his elbow and pointed at the stage. He whispered something and started to giggle. She spotted Ginny Piccolo, who spotted her back and stuck out her tongue. She even saw Hatchet Hackerman, who had stopped by on her way to the airport. Then she saw Mr. Finelli. He winked and smiled.

Mindy swallowed hard. She heard Frankie's words. She remembered everything that had happened, from the food fight to the locker room. She thought about it, and started to rap.

*Clap-snap. Clap-snap. Clap-snap-clap!*

> *"Our teacher's so mean,*
> *He bathes in witches' brew.*
> *We think he's a monster . . ."*

Mindy stopped rapping. She couldn't stop thinking. She looked at Frankie, Samantha, and Jeff. They all nodded. Mindy hesitated, then started to rap again.

*Clap-snap. Clap-snap. Clap-snap-clap!*

> *"Our teacher's not mean.*
> *He's really pretty cool.*
> *We thought he was monster,*
> *But that's, like, April fool."*

*Clap-snap. Clap-snap. Clap-snap-clap!*

Mindy continued on with the second verse:

> *"This essay's our chance*
> *To bring the story out.*
> *So hold on to your pants*
> *And hear us proudly shout."*

**113**

Mindy held up her hands. Everyone knew she wanted to do the first chorus on her own.

> *"Mis-ter Finelli.*
> *You know he can teach.*
> *He's on our case both day and night*
> *'Cause he's a teaching crea . . . ture."*

*Clap-snap. Clap-snap. Clap-snap-clap!*
Jeff changed his verse:

> *"Mis-ter Finelli.*
> *You know he ain't sleazy.*
> *He really can teach us.*
> *You know that ain't easy."*

The whole class joined in on the *Clap-snap. Clap-snap. Clap-snap-clap!*
Samantha stepped in front of the microphone.

> *"He's one fine teacher.*
> *He plays the Golden Rule.*
> *Shout it from the bleacher.*
> *He's the best in our school."*

*Clap-snap. Clap-snap. Clap-snap-clap!*
Mindy, Frankie, Jeff, and Samantha all joined in the chorus:

*"Mis-ter Finelli.*
  *You know he can teach.*
  *He's on our case both day and night*
  *'Cause he's a teaching crea . . . ture."*

*Clap-snap. Clap-snap. Clap-snap-clap!*
Mindy took the next verse:

  *"He taught us about Napoleon.*
  *We love his friend named Max.*
  *The learning keeps on rollin' in.*
  *He fills our heads with facts."*

*Clap-snap. Clap-snap. Clap-snap-clap!*
Frankie smiled broadly. He'd figured out his new verse:

  *"He should be our teacher.*
  *He can help us pass.*
  *If anyone says different,*
  *I hope that they get gas."*

*Clap-snap. Clap-snap. Clap-snap-clap!*
This time the entire class joined in the chorus:

  *"Mis-ter Finelli.*
  *You know he can teach.*

**115**

*He's on our case both day and night*
*'Cause he's a teaching crea . . . ture."*

*Clap-snap. Clap-snap. Clap-snap-clap!*

Just as they'd rehearsed it, each person took one line in the final verse. Jeff rapped the first, followed by Frankie, Samantha, and finally Mindy:

*"He's the best teacher."*
*"No ifs. No ands. No doubt."*
*"We want him to know it."*
*"That's what this rap's about."*

*Clap-snap. Clap-snap. Clap-snap-clap!*

Again, as at rehearsal, the sixth-graders in Mr. Finelli's class made fish faces and pretended to swim off the stage after the last clap. Why ruin a great ending?

After a moment of stunned silence, everyone in the audience began applauding. Except for one man in a toupee, who was standing up and cheering.

# Chapter Fourteen

**Ten sixth-grade classes** had competed in the essay contest. Mr. Finelli's finished ninth. The judges said that while they liked the class's creativity, they felt a rap didn't really qualify as an essay.

Mr. Nowak's class finished tenth. His was the last class to deliver an essay. When the students got onstage, one boy walked up to the microphone and said, "Essay subject: What We Like About Our Teacher." Then Mr. Nowak's entire class shouted "Nothing!" and walked off the stage and out of the school.

Even though they didn't come in first, a week after the contest Mr. Finelli threw his class a pizza party. To pay off his bet, Mr. Nowak had to serve the pizza and shave his eyebrows.

About halfway through the party, when everyone

was happily scarfing down pizza, there was a loud splash. The whole class turned and watched as a mass of brown hair slowly sank to the bottom of the fish tank.

Mr. Finelli walked over to Mindy. The classroom light reflected off the top of his head. "Miss Collins," he said. "Would you do me just one itty-bitty favor?"

"Ooooo-kay," Mindy said warily, worrying about what Mr. Finelli might ask her to do.

"Great," Mr. Finelli said happily. "Would you please pass me a slice of pizza?"

Mindy and Mr. Finelli slapped high fives as Mr. Finelli turned to Mr. Nowak. "There's one more thing I need you to do to pay off our bet. Remember, you said *anything.*"

"All right, what is it?" Mr. Nowak demanded. The teacher was in a really grumpy mood that was about to become even grumpier.

Mr. Finelli smiled. "Would you please get my hair?"

# About the Author

**Jerry Piasecki** is the creative director for a Michigan advertising agency. Previously he was a radio newsperson in Detroit and New York. He has also written, directed, and acted in numerous commercials, industrial films, and documentaries. The writing he loves most, though, is for young readers, "where one is free to let the mind soar beyond grown-up barriers and defenses." Jerry lives in Farmington Hills, Michigan. He has a fifteen-year-old daughter, Amanda, who has a dog named Rusty and a cat named Pepper.